TAMING
THE LAST ST CLAIRE

TAMING
THE LAST ST CLAIRE

BY

CAROLE MORTIMER

MILLS
BOON®

To everyone who has enjoyed the St Claires
as much as I have!

CHAPTER ONE

'So, ARE you going to stand there all morning looking down your superior nose at me, or are you going to do something useful and offer to carry one of these boxes up in the lift for me?'

Gideon closed his eyes. Counted to ten. Slowly. Breathed in. And then out again. Even more slowly. Before once again opening his eyes.

No, Joey McKinley was still there. In fact she had straightened from bending over the boot of her car, parked two bays down from Gideon's own in this private underground car park, and was now peremptorily tapping the sole of one three-inch stiletto-heeled shoe against the concrete floor. He knew this woman would become the bane of his existence for the next four weeks, if this situation was allowed to continue.

Joey McKinley. Twenty-eight years old, five foot four inches tall, with short, silky red hair that somehow wisped up and away from the heart-shaped beauty of her face, challenging jade-green eyes, and a creamily smooth complexion with a soft sprinkling of freckles across the bridge of her tiny nose, her lips full and sensual. The leanness of her obviously physically fit body was shown to advantage in a smart black tailored business suit and a silk blouse the same jade-green colour as her eyes.

'Well?' his own personal nemesis challenged, that impatient tapping of her shoe against the concrete floor increasing as she looked across at him with auburn brows arched over those mocking green eyes.

Gideon drew in another deep and steadying breath as he considered the numerous ways in which he might cause his older brother Lucan pain for having placed him in this untenable position in the first place. Not enough to do any serious damage, of course. But a *little* pain? Gideon felt no qualms whatsoever about that. Lucan obviously felt a similar lack of concern about Gideon's welfare, having inflicted this woman on him without a second's consideration.

It was something Gideon had been contemplating for the last thirty-six hours, in fact. Ever since Lucan had informed him, at his wedding reception on Saturday evening, that when Gideon took over as temporary chairman of the St Claire Corporation for the month that he and Lexie were away on their honeymoon, he had arranged for Joey McKinley to take Gideon's place as the company's legal representative.

Gideon's assurances that he was perfectly capable of fulfilling both roles had made absolutely no impact on his older brother. He'd also ignored Gideon when he'd confessed he had his doubts that he and Joey McKinley could work together.

Gideon respected the woman as a lawyer, having heard only positive comments from other colleagues concerning her ability in a courtroom, but on every other level she succeeded in making his hackles rise.

That red hair was like a shining beacon in any room she happened to be in, and she had a husky and sensual laugh that, when released, had every male head in the vicinity turning in her direction. She had been wearing a dress the last two times Gideon had met her—firstly, an ankle-length sheath of a maid of honour gown in a deep jade colour at her sister Stephanie and his brother Jordan's wedding, almost two months ago, and a red knee-length dress at Lucan and Lexie's wedding on Saturday. The latter should have clashed with the bright copper cap of her hair, but instead it had just seemed to emphasise the natural gold and cinnamon highlights running through those strands.

The black business suit she was wearing today should have looked crisp and professional, but somehow...didn't. The jacket was short and figure-hugging, and the top three buttons left unfastened on the green silk blouse she wore beneath enabled him to see the tops of full and creamy breasts. The fitted knee-length skirt showed off an expanse of her shapely legs.

In other words, Joey McKinley was—

'You know, I've seen paint dry quicker than you appear to be able to make up your mind!' she called out.

—a veritable thorn in his side!

He drew in another controlling breath in an effort to force the tension from his body. 'Do you always have to be this abrasive?' Silly question; he knew her well enough by now to know that she always said exactly what happened to be on her mind at the time. Something that Gideon, a man who always measured his words carefully before speaking, found disturbing to say the least.

Her next comment was a prime example of that bluntness. 'Maybe I wouldn't feel the need if you occasionally took that I'm-so-superior stick out of your backside and joined the rest of us mortals in the real world.'

Gideon winced. The two of them had met— what?—four times in total. Most recently two days ago, at Lucan and Lexie's wedding, and before that nine weeks ago, when he'd first met her in her office at Pickard, Pickard and Wright, after he had gone to inform her he had managed to extricate her twin sister Stephanie from an awkward legal situation. Two weeks after that he'd met her at the wedding rehearsal of his twin brother Jordan and Stephanie, and then he'd seen her again at their wedding a week later.

Gideon frowned now as he remembered his absolute astonishment during Jordan and Stephanie's marriage ceremony. Everything had gone so smoothly in the lead-up to the wedding, and Gideon, as his brother's best man, had ensured that he and Jordan arrived at the church in plenty of time. Gideon had even felt a lump of emotion in his own throat, on his twin's behalf, when the two of them had turned to see how beautiful Stephanie looked as she walked down the aisle. Until, that was, Gideon had caught the look of derision in Joey's gaze as she'd glanced at him from where she followed just behind her twin.

Not that this was anything unusual; the two of them seemed to have taken an instant dislike to each other the very first time they'd met. No, the reason for Gideon's astonishment had come later in the ceremony, when everyone had sat down while Jordan and Stephanie and their two witnesses signed the register, and he'd heard an angel singing.

A single, unaccompanied voice had soared majestically to the heavens, filling the church to the rafters, as sweet and clear as the perfect, melodic chiming of a bell.

He had never before heard anything so beautiful as that voice—so clear and plaintive it had been almost magical as it claimed his emotions.

He had felt so dazed, his senses so completely captivated by the pure and haunting beauty of that voice, that it had taken him a minute or so to realise that all the wedding guests were looking towards the right side of the church—which was when Gideon had realised that the singing 'angel' was none other than Joey McKinley!

Joey had no idea why it was that Gideon St Claire brought out the very worst in her—to the extent that she enjoyed nothing more than deliberately baiting him out of what she considered his arrogant complacency. Maybe it really *was* that superior attitude of his that bugged her. Or the fact that, with his icy reserve firmly clamped in place, he was always so emotionally unresponsive. Everything about him was restrained, from the short style of his wonderful gold-coloured hair, the tailored dark suits he wore—always over a white shirt and matched with a discreetly subdued silk tie—to the expensive but unremarkable metallic-grey saloon car he drove. If Joey had been as rich as the St Claire family was reputed to be then she would have driven a sporty red Ferrari at the very least!

Or her resentment *could* just stem from the fact that a couple of months ago Gideon St Claire had stepped in, with his highly polished size eleven handmade leather shoes, and sorted out a delicate and personal legal matter for her sister, which Joey had been trying—unsuccessfully—to settle for weeks.

It certainly couldn't have anything to do with the fact that, putting the icy reserve apart, the man was as handsome as sin but gave every impression he hadn't so much as noticed Joey was a female, let alone a passably attractive one!

His hair—cut too short for her liking—was the colour and texture of spun gold, and styled over his ears and brow. His eyes were a dark and piercing brown, set in a ruggedly handsome face, and as if that wasn't enough, nature had bestowed upon him high cheekbones, sensually chiselled lips, and an arrogantly square jaw.

Having studied him from beneath lowered lashes at their second meeting—she had been too overwhelmed by both his legal reputation and his considerable arrogance the first time they met in her office!—Joey had no doubt, just from the predatory way that he moved, that the body beneath those dark tailored suits and white silk shirts was powerfully lean and muscled.

Wheat-gold hair, chocolate-brown eyes, broodingly sensual features that any male model would kill for, and a body that was all hard masculine contours meant that Gideon St Claire was seriously hot—with a capital H. A description that, if he were to hear it, would no doubt offend all his icily reserved sensibilities!

Taking all that smouldering sensuality into consideration, Joey had been intrigued by the fact that he hadn't brought a woman with him to the weddings of his brothers. That coupled with the fact that Gideon didn't even seem to register her as a female, had eventually made Joey ask her sister whether Gideon maybe preferred men to women. She had assumed Stephanie's answer to be a resounding *no* after it had taken her sister almost five minutes to stop laughing hysterically.

So, Mr Arrogantly Reserved and Broodingly Sensual obviously liked women—just not Joey!

Well, that was fine with her—Gideon St Claire might be one of the most disturbingly attractive men Joey had ever met, but the lack of interest he always showed in her only succeeded in making her feel defensive, and more often than not she deliberately set out to shock him.

'Are you suffering from laryngitis, or are you just not a morning person?' The bright cheerfulness with which Joey spoke showed neither of those two things applied to her.

'Perhaps if you were to stop talking long enough to allow me to answer you?' He spoke tersely, yet even the low and gravelly tenor of his voice was sexy, she thought with a mental sigh. He made no move to close the short distance between their two parked cars. 'Miss McKinley—'

'Joey.'

His nostrils flared with obvious distaste. 'Would you object if I were to call you Josephine?'

'Not at all—as long as you don't mind me reacting the same way I did the last time someone tried to do that,' she came back breezily. 'He ended up with a black eye,' she supplied with a smile as Gideon raised questioning blond brows.

One of those brows remained raised. 'You don't like the name Josephine?'

'Obviously not.'

This was not going well, Gideon accepted heavily. He had come to the conclusion, during the hours since Lucan had spoken to him on Saturday evening, that the only solution to this problem was for him to talk to Joey and calmly and logically explain why he didn't feel they could work together, before waving her a cheery goodbye and getting on with his role of acting chairman of the St Claire Corporation. For heaven's sake, she must be as aware as he was of their different approaches to—well, *everything*!

A reasonable and well thought out plan, he had believed at the time. Until he had actually been faced with the abrasively outspoken woman in person. Just these few minutes of conversation with her was enough to show him that his conclusion had been entirely correct. However, he'd also swiftly realised that any suggestion on his part that she might care to rethink agreeing to work with him for a month would probably only result in the contrary Joey McKinley doing the exact opposite.

For once in Gideon's well-ordered life he had no idea what to do or say to best achieve his objective. He just knew he couldn't tolerate working in close proximity with this forthright young woman for four weeks and stay sane!

Even if she did have the singing voice of an angel...

The fact that Lucan had announced he was taking a whole month off for his honeymoon, during which he intended to be completely incommunicado except for absolute emergencies, was extraordinary in itself.

Not that Gideon should have been surprised—both his brothers had been behaving in a completely unpredictable manner since they had met and as quickly married the two women they had fallen in love with. It wasn't that he didn't like both Stephanie and Lexie—he did. It was the change in his two brothers that he found... unsettling.

Jordan, an A-list actor who had enjoyed any number of relationships with beautiful actresses and models during the past ten years, had surprisingly fallen in love with his physiotherapist two months ago, and showed every appearance of continuing to be totally besotted with Stephanie now the two of them were married. To the extent that the filming of his current movie was completely scheduled around the hours Stephanie worked at the clinic she had opened since moving to LA.

And until Lucan had met and fallen in love with Lexie he had never taken more than a few days away from the company he had built up into one of the most diverse and successful in the world. In fact, *driven* was the word Gideon would most have associated with his older brother until the advent of Lexie into his life only a few short weeks ago.

It was a word that could have been associated with all three of the St Claire brothers since they'd reached adulthood and entered their chosen professions: Gideon in law, Jordan in acting, Lucan in the world of business.

All of that had changed in the past two months, and as a man who preferred order and continuity Gideon was still trying to come to terms with it. Something he wasn't likely to do with the annoying Joey McKinley haunting his every working moment!

'Very well, then. Joey it is.' He gave an almost imperceptible sigh. 'I'm sure that Pickard, Pickard and Wright—Jason Pickard, in particular—was sorry to see you go.'

'See me go where, exactly?'

Gideon eyed her impatiently. Really, nothing he had heard about this woman had ever given him reason to question her intelligence. '*Here*, of course.'

Joey looked taken aback. 'I'm sorry, but you'll have to explain what you mean. Especially the "Jason Pickard, in particular" remark,' she added coolly.

Gideon wasn't enjoying having this personal conversation in the middle of a private car park, of all places, where any of the other company employees might arrive at any moment. Admittedly it was only a little after eight o'clock in the morning, and most St Claire Corporation employees didn't arrive until nearly nine o'clock, but it would be most unprofessional for anyone to arrive early and see the acting chairman at loggerheads with an unknown woman in the car park.

Gideon closed the distance between them in three long strides, to stand only feet away from Joey, and instantly became uncomfortably aware of the light but heady perfume she wore. The choice of perfume was a surprise; Gideon would have thought, with her forceful personality, that she would wear one of those I'm-here-notice-me perfumes. The type of perfume that tended to give Gideon a headache the moment he inhaled. Instead, it was a delicate, subtly sensuous scent that made him react in an immediate way he intended to ignore.

His mouth thinned. 'I was merely trying to express my sympathy at how unreasonable it was of Lucan to ask you to give up your place at Pickard, Pickard and Wright in order to work here for only four weeks.'

Joey found herself momentarily distracted as she watched Gideon move, with the lean and predatory grace of a jungle cat.

Once again she considered it a perfect waste of a gorgeous man that he was as tightly buttoned down as the points on the collar of his pristine white shirt. A little effort on Gideon's part— and fewer disapproving looks!—and the man wouldn't only be arrogantly handsome but also totally devastating to any female with a pulse and a heartbeat.

If he would just grow his hair a little longer he would look younger, and also rakishly sexy. Ditto as regards those conservative tailored suits he always wore. Put him in a pair of faded jeans and a figure-hugging black T-shirt, to show off his muscled chest and arms, and any woman with red blood in her veins was likely to have an orgasm just looking at him!

Joey smiled wickedly to herself, imagining the look of horror that would no doubt come over his arrogantly handsome face if he were even to *guess* at the inappropriateness of the thoughts she was having about him.

'Do you find something amusing?'

It *was* amusing to imagine a more relaxed and sexy Gideon St Claire, as he attempted to fend off the attentions of all those panting women! But it was not so funny that Joey was actually aware of how much more dangerously attractive this man could be if he would just lighten up a little…

She gave herself a mental shake as she looked up into that darkly disapproving face; this man really wasn't her type. She preferred men with the daring and energy to try anything new; Gideon gave the impression that the last new thing he had tried was wearing black socks instead of grey!

She drew in a deep breath. 'Oh, but I haven't given up my place at Pickard, Pickard and Wright; the senior partners were only too happy to give me a month's leave of absence so I can help Lucan out.'

Something, Gideon realised with rising impatience, that must have taken some time to arrange. 'Exactly *when* did Lucan make all these arrangements?'

'Three weeks ago—' Joey broke off to look up at him with narrowed, assessing eyes. 'When did Lucan break the bad news to *you*?'

Gideon stiffened. 'I don't remember saying I regard it as bad news.'

'You implied it,' she dismissed shortly. 'So—when?'

His jaw tightened. 'I really don't see—'

'He only told you at the wedding on Saturday, didn't he?' she realised slowly.

Gideon had absolutely no idea why it was he always felt less in control of the situation around this particular woman. During his years in a courtroom he knew he'd acquired a reputation for being formidable. Now, as a corporate lawyer for Lucan's vast companies worldwide, he knew he was regarded as being no less ruthless than his older brother. And yet just having a conversation with the unpredictable Joey McKinley was enough to set his teeth on edge. To set the *whole* of him on edge, in fact…

'He did, didn't he?' Joey said with satisfaction, those green eyes now openly laughing at him. 'It probably totally ruined the rest of your weekend, too!'

Gideon's fingers tightened about the handle of his black briefcase. 'My weekend was perfectly enjoyable, thank you,' he lied stiffly. 'In fact I had lunch with Stephanie and Jordan yesterday, as they are flying back to LA early today.'

'And I had breakfast with them this morning, before driving them to the airport, and neither of them mentioned you'd asked for my telephone number. Which I'd have thought you *would* have done if you had wanted to have this conversation with me earlier.' Joey McKinley gave a taunting shake of her head.

It *had* crossed Gideon's mind, in fact, to ask

Stephanie for her sister's private telephone number, but on consideration he had decided not to involve either of their families in what was, after all, a private clash of personalities.

'Or maybe you just didn't want either of them to jump to the wrong conclusions?'

He scowled his displeasure. 'I beg your pardon?'

'By you asking for my home telephone number. I'm sure you wouldn't have wanted to give Steph and Jordan the impression that you have a personal interest in me,' she answered mockingly.

Gideon drew in yet another deep, controlling breath—a futile exercise, he thought wryly. He couldn't remember feeling as rattled as this in a long time. 'I believe that's very unlikely.'

'You do?'

Was it his imagination, or was Joey suddenly standing closer than she had been a few seconds ago? So close that Gideon could actually see the full swell of her breasts and the top of the lacy cup of her bra, and the pulse beating smoothly, enticingly, at the base of her throat.

Dear Lord…

His gaze turned to ice. 'Surely you recognise

just from this conversation that we can't possibly work together?'

She was suddenly all business again as she straightened. 'My arrangement is with Lucan, Gideon—not you. And I make a point of never letting people down once I've agreed to do something. A character trait I believe you share?'

It appeared that Joey was as aware of parts of Gideon's nature as he was of hers! 'I'm sure that Pickard, Pickard and Wright are more in need of your professional skills than I am,' he pointed out smoothly.

'On the contrary, they were only too happy to accommodate Lucan's request,' she assured him.

Of course they were, he thought derisively. No doubt Pickard, Pickard and Wright were perfectly aware of the prestige of allowing one of their associates to work at the St Claire Corporation for a month. Being asked for personally by a man of Lucan St Claire's standing in the business world wouldn't do Joey McKinley's career any harm, either.

'So, Gideon, Lucan's happy with the arrangement, Pickard, Pickard and Wright are happy with the arrangement and I'm happy with the arrangement—it appears *you're* the only one who isn't.' She looked him straight in the eye—an obvious challenge.

Gideon coldly returned that gaze. 'I don't recall saying I was unhappy with it.'

'No?'

'No.'

'Then that little problem appears to have been settled to everyone's satisfaction, doesn't it,' she dismissed lightly.

Like hell it was! As far as Gideon was concerned, having Joey in the St Claire building for the next four weeks was totally unacceptable.

She cut into his dire thoughts with another equally unwelcome sally. 'Perhaps now you would care to explain exactly what you meant when you commented that "Jason Pickard, in particular" would have been sorry to see me go?'

Gideon realised she wasn't being deliberately provocative any more. Her emotions were now much more subtle. On the surface she sounded pleasantly interested, but he recognised the anger burning beneath that supposedly calm surface;

it was there in the sparkling green of her eyes and the flush to those creamy cheeks. Although why she should feel that way Gideon had no idea; everyone in the close-knit law community knew that she had been involved with the junior Pickard for the past six months.

He shrugged broad shoulders. 'It's public knowledge that the two of you are friends.'

'That's exactly what we are—*friends*,' she stated evenly. 'Nothing more, nothing less.'

'I apologise if I've stepped on your personal toes.'

'I've just told you that you haven't,' she said.

Gideon's mouth thinned. 'I'm not prepared to get into an argument with you over a perfectly innocent remark which I have already apologised for.'

'Does anyone ever dare to argue with you, Gideon?' Joey McKinley eyed him with obvious frustration.

'Obviously,' he drawled, looking at her pointedly.

'This isn't an argument, Gideon, it's a dialogue,' she snapped.

He shook his head. 'I really don't have time for this, so if you wouldn't mind—'

'But I *do* mind, Gideon.' She was suddenly standing much too close to him again as she interrupted him ruthlessly. So close that he could feel the warmth of her breath against his jaw as the three-inch stiletto heels on her shoes brought the top of her head to his eye level.

Gideon dearly wished he had never started this conversation. That he had just picked up one of the boxes from the boot of this woman's bright red Mini and travelled up in the lift with her, before shutting himself away for the day in Lucan's office.

He was thirty-four years old, successful in his chosen career, and the brief and businesslike affairs he occasionally indulged in rarely even registered on the scale of his emotions. Other than the affection Gideon felt for his two brothers and his mother, he preferred to keep a physical and emotional distance from the rest of humanity.

It was difficult to do that around the forceful Joey McKinley. Especially when she was now so close to him that he could smell the lemon of her shampoo, and see the auburn, gold and cinnamon highlights in that glossy red hair. An unusual colour that Gideon knew didn't come out of a bottle, because her twin sister had hair with exactly the same beautiful autumn shades.

What would that hair feel like to touch? As soft and silky as it looked? Or as brittle and defensive as the woman herself—

Gideon took an abrupt step back, shutting down his thoughts as he realised what he was doing, his jaw tight as he looked down the length of his nose at her. 'Joey, I appreciate the fact that your sister being married to my brother puts us in the position of being almost related.' *Almost* being the operative word! 'But let me state here and now that I have absolutely no interest in knowing anything about your sex life.'

Joey's eyed widened at the vehemence she heard in Gideon's tone. She had no doubt that he genuinely respected and liked her sister, and that he approved of Stephanie's marriage to his brother. So why had he decided he disliked Joey from their very first meeting?

Maybe he had disliked and disapproved of her *before* that first meeting, if his assumptions about her friendship with Jason Pickard were any indication, she mused. She was well aware of the rumours that had circulated about her and the junior partner at Pickard, Pickard and Wright for the past six months. Erroneous rumours, as it happened.

Oh, Jason was incredibly handsome, and the two of them went out to dinner at least once a week. Joey always enjoyed herself on those evenings as she found Jason good company. But their friendship wasn't based on either sexual attraction or love.

In actual fact their friendship had become more in the nature of a smokescreen, because Jason was really in love with a man he had met at university and had shared an apartment with for the past ten years. Unfortunately his parents, Pickard Senior and Gloria, had no idea that their son's relationship with the other man was anything more than friendship, and would have vehemently disapproved if they did.

Joey had been thrilled the first time Jason had asked her out—after all, he was the second Pickard in Pickard, Pickard and Wright. But it hadn't taken her long to realise that Jason wasn't in the least sexually interested in her. With her usual straightforwardness she had asked a couple of blunt questions, and eventually received a couple of straight answers. The revelation about Jason's sexuality hadn't changed anything as far as Joey was concerned; she liked him and enjoyed his company. Enough to agree to go out to dinner with him often—and why not, when there was very little happening in her own love life at the moment! And so the myth of their having a relationship had been born, a myth, it seemed, that even the coldly aloof Gideon St Claire was aware of...

Joey gave him a cool smile. 'Then why are we still standing here discussing my sex life?'

'You—' Gideon broke off in obvious frustration, choosing instead to exercise rigid self-control. 'Shall we just take your things upstairs and get to work?' He moved to pick up one of the boxes from the boot of her car before walking stiffly over to the private lift.

Joey picked up the other box and then closed the boot and locked her car, a smile of satisfaction curving her lips as she followed him.

The next four weeks—if they entailed

shaking Gideon St Claire out of his aloof com-placency—promised to be a lot of fun. For her, if not for himself...

CHAPTER TWO

'WHERE are you going?' Gideon questioned sharply as he turned and saw that, instead of following him down the hallway to his own office, Joey had stopped outside the office usually reserved for Lucan's PA. It wasn't currently occupied, because Lexie had become Lucan's PA three weeks ago, and the two of them were now happily honeymooning together on a private Caribbean island for a month.

Mocking green eyes met his. 'I believe it was an attempt at diplomacy on Lucan's part when he suggested I might like to use Lexie's vacant office rather than your own.'

After the bombshell Lucan had dropped on Gideon at the wedding reception on Saturday evening, he didn't have too much faith in his older brother's 'diplomacy'!

'And how did you *know* that particular office was Lexie's?'

'You mean apart from the fact her name is printed on the door?'

Gideon scowled darkly at Joey's obvious sarcasm. 'Apart from that, yes,' he gritted out.

She shrugged slender shoulders. 'I came over on Thursday afternoon, so that Lucan could explain exactly what it is he wants me to do while he and Lexie are away.'

Thursday afternoon. The one afternoon in the week when Gideon didn't work at the St Claire Corporation but instead went to the small office he kept across town and dealt with private legal matters needing his attention. A fact that Lucan would have been well aware of, damn him.

Maybe Gideon had been overly generous concerning that 'little' amount of pain he had considered inflicting on his older brother the next time he saw him!

'And exactly what *is* it he wants you to do here while he and Lexie are away?' Besides be a damned nuisance to him, of course!

Joey shrugged. 'Well, Lucan seemed to have a pretty good idea that you aren't going to release too much of the legal side of things to me.' Those jade-green eyes danced knowingly. 'But obviously I'll be only too happy to take up the slack. There's also the fact that with Lexie away too you're without a PA.'

'My own secretary—'

'Is now *my* secretary,' she reminded him pertly.

Damn it, this situation was just getting worse—made even more so by the fact that he suspected Lucan and Lexie were sitting on their private Caribbean island right now having a really good laugh at his expense. Falling in love hadn't just made his older brother unpredictable; it had also brought out a distinctly warped sense of humour in him!

'If you would prefer, I can use your office rather than this one,' Joey said as she once again tapped the toe of one stiletto-heeled shoe to mark her impatience. 'Could you make your mind up soon, Gideon; this box is getting heavy!'

His mouth pursed with frustration. He had always thought of the office down the hallway as being his own personal space: all wood-panelled walls, floor to ceiling bookshelves containing his reference books on English and foreign law, all in alphabetical order. And the top of his mahogany desk was always completely cleared at the end of each working day, with none of the personal clutter that so many people seemed to surround themselves with during working hours.

The two bursting boxes they had carried upstairs seemed to imply Joey intended surrounding herself with exactly that sort of reprehensible clutter for the next four weeks, he mused. No, he *didn't* relish the idea of having his office personalised by this woman. But knowing that Joey McKinley's disturbing presence was in the office next door to the one he intended using would be just as unacceptable—

'Too late,' Joey announced decisively, and she lowered the door handle to Lexie's office with her elbow before breezing inside. 'Very nice,' she could be heard murmuring appreciatively.

Gideon reluctantly followed her into the office Lucan had decorated before Lexie became his permanent PA three weeks ago, seeing again that the desk of mellow pine, the cream walls and gold-coloured carpet were all a perfect foil for Lexie's long black hair.

But he couldn't help noticing against his will that they were equally complementary to Joey's rich auburn-gold-cinnamon-red hair and jade green eyes...

'What on earth do you have in here—rocks?' Gideon muttered bad-temperedly as he crossed the room to drop the box he was carrying down onto the desktop beside Joey's own.

Not a happy bunny, she recognised ruefully as she saw his dark scowl. Not a bunny at all, actually. No, as Gideon began to prowl restlessly about the office he looked more like the predator Joey had likened him to earlier...

'Not quite,' she answered, as she flipped up the lid of one of the boxes to start taking out the objects and unwrapping them from protective newspaper.

The usual predictable clutter, Gideon recognised. Her law degree. A couple of framed photographs—one of her parents, the other of Stephanie and Jordan at their wedding. A paperweight with a perfect yellow rose inside. A golden dragon.

Hold on a minute—*a golden dragon*?

'Yes?' Joey continued to hold the small golden ornament almost defensively in the palm of her hand as she turned to look at him.

It was Gideon's first indication that he had actually made an exclamation out loud. But, damn it, a *dragon*! Even one as romantically beautiful as this—with the creature's scaled body beautifully etched in gold, its wings extended as if it were about to take flight, and two small yellow sapphires set in the fierceness of its face for eyes—didn't quite fit in with the abrasive image he had formed of this woman.

Any more than that angelic singing voice, he suddenly recalled.

Joey looked across at him and frowned; really, you would think from his disgusted expression that she had just produced a semi-automatic rifle and intended mounting it on the wall!

'Stephanie had this made for me when I got my law degree.'

Her twin had always known that the dragon meant something to Joey. A golden dragon had been a feature in Joey's dreams since she was seven years old. Whenever she'd had a problem—difficulties at school, or with friends—and when she and Stephanie were ten and had been involved in the car accident that had left her twin unable to walk for two years, Joey had dreamt of her golden dragon and instantly felt reassured that everything would work out.

Consequently, where she went, this dragon went too.

She placed it firmly in the centre of the empty desk. 'It has great sentimental value.'

'If Stephanie gave it to you, then I'm sure it does.' Gideon acknowledged softly.

Joey looked up at him, looking for this man's usual cold distance whenever he spoke to her. Instead she sensed almost an affinity... 'Do you miss Jordan?'

Gideon looked taken aback by the question. 'There's hardly been time for that when he only left this morning.'

'I meant before that, of course,' Joey said impatiently. 'He's been in LA how long now?'

He frowned. 'Ten years.'

Stephanie had only been gone for two months, but Joey was still deeply aware of the void her twin had left in her own life. 'Did you miss him when he first left?'

'You're still missing Stephanie?'

'There's no need to sound so surprised, Gideon,' she said ruefully.

Gideon *was* surprised, and yet he knew he shouldn't have been. Just because Joey appeared to enjoy mocking him at every opportunity, there was absolutely no reason for him to assume she didn't have the same deep emotional connection to her own twin that he had with Jordan.

'Yes, I missed Jordan very much when he first went to LA,' he acknowledged gruffly. 'It does get easier,' he added.

The two of them stared across the office at each other for several long minutes. As if each recognised something in the other that they hadn't been aware of before. A softness. A chink in their armour. A vulnerability...

Whilst Gideon found this insight into Joey's emotions faintly disturbing, he found it even more so in himself; revealing vulnerability of any kind was not something Gideon did. *Ever.*

'The dragon is very beautiful,' he said, in a swift change of subject. 'But personally I prefer to believe in the things I can see and touch,' he added.

'Maybe that's your problem,' Joey said as she turned away to continue unpacking the contents of the box.

Gideon's jaw tightened. 'I wasn't aware that I *had* a problem.'

Joey raised auburn brows as she sat on the edge of the desk behind her, her pencil-slim skirt hitching up slightly as she did so, exposing more of her shapely legs. 'You don't see the fact that you have absolutely no imagination as being a problem?'

Gideon ignored that bare expanse of skin and kept his gaze firmly fixed on her beautiful heart-shaped face. 'I have always found basing my opinions on cold, hard reality to be the better option.'

'Don't you mean the boring, unimaginative option?' she taunted.

'I believe I know myself well enough to know exactly what I mean, Joey.' He glared down at her.

Joey had regretted telling him how much she still missed Stephanie almost as soon as she had started the conversation. But she had been sur-prised when Gideon admitted missing his own twin just as much.

He gave every impression of being self-contained. A cold and unsentimental man. To imagine him feeling the same ache of loneliness for his own twin as she felt for Stephanie suddenly made him seem all too human.

But perhaps he felt the same about her? The thought suddenly seemed much too intimate. 'There's no need to get your boxers in a twist, Gideon,' she murmured, being deliberately provocative to hide her uneasiness.

'My boxers?' Gideon's nostrils flared in distaste.

'That's always supposing you *wear* boxers, of course,' Joey continued outrageously. 'Yet I somehow can't see you going commando—'

'I would prefer that we not discuss my underwear, or lack of it, if you don't mind,' he bit out with an incredulous shake of his head. 'You really are the most irritating woman I have ever met.'

'Really?' Joey smiled appreciatively.

Gideon eyed her in exasperation. 'It wasn't meant as a compliment!'

'I didn't think for one moment that it was,' she said dryly. 'But can I help it if I feel honoured that the coolly aloof Gideon St Claire has lowered his aristocratic brown eyes far enough to even notice my existence, let alone to actually form an opinion about me?'

Gideon realised it was this woman's impulsiveness that made him feel so uneasy in her company. So unsure and definitely wary of what she was going to do or say next. It wasn't a comfortable admission from a man who usually maintained a tight control over his own emotions. Not comfortable at all...

His mouth compressed into a hard line. 'Now who's being insulting?'

'Was I?' she came back airily. 'But you *do* have brown eyes. And you *are* an aristocrat. Lord Gideon St Claire, to be exact,' she added, as though he'd forgotten.

Neither he, nor his two brothers ever used their titles. In fact most people were completely unaware that Lucan was the current Duke of Stourbridge, or that his younger twin brothers were both lords. A fact that Joey was well aware of.

Instead of answering her, Gideon glanced down at the plain gold watch on his wrist. 'I'm afraid I don't have any more time to waste on this. I have an appointment at nine o'clock.'

She smiled unabashedly. 'Does that mean the welcome speech—you know…the usual *glad to have you with us, don't hesitate to ask if you need anything, blah, blah, blah*—is now over?'

Gideon drew in a harsh breath. Both of them knew there had been no welcome speech from him at all—not even a brief, unenthusiastic one. Which was obviously the whole point of her remark.

'I'm sure you're fully aware by now that I would be happier not to have you working here at all,' he said honestly.

'Life can be cruel that way, can't it?' she said, her smile undimmed.

Gideon gave her one last frustrated frown, before turning on his heel and going into the adjoining office and all but slamming the door closed behind him.

Joey's breath left her lungs in a relieved whoosh once she was alone in Lexie's office. That last conversation about Gideon's underwear had no doubt completely restored the opinion he'd obviously held of her *before* her earlier lapse in admitting that she deeply missed Stephanie.

Joey was well aware of what people thought

of her lawyer persona—aggressive, forceful, too outspoken. She was a shark circling her prey when she defended her client in a courtroom— and it was a reputation she had deliberately nurtured.

Not too many people were ever allowed to see past that veneer of professional toughness to the real Joey beneath, as Gideon had when she'd talked of missing her twin…

Joey had deliberately donned her professional toughness a couple of years ago, after one too many slights, because she was a woman in the male-dominated career she had chosen to enter. And after one too many men, less capable than she believed herself to be, had been given jobs because of their gender rather than their ability. The third time Joey had been passed over in that way was when she had decided that if she couldn't beat them then she was going to join them and beat them at their own game.

Consequently, before she went for her interview at Pickard, Pickard and Wright two years ago, Joey had gone out and bought herself half a dozen of what she considered to be power suits, had had her hair styled unfemininely short, and adopted an abrasive and aggressive personality to match. The changes had proved to be successful, and she had managed to land the job with that prestigious firm of lawyers.

Once she had been given the job Joey had softened her attitude and appearance slightly, recognising that in some circumstances femininity—showing a little cleavage and wearing stiletto-heeled shoes for example—could be just as effective as abrasive aggression.

But she couldn't say she was altogether comfortable with the fact that her highly professional persona had slipped slightly when she had been talking with Gideon St Claire.

'I'm taking a break now, and going to the coffee shop down the street to get a hot chocolate. Do you want anything while I'm there?'

Gideon scowled his irritation as he looked up from the figures he had been studying on his computer screen to where Joey stood in the now open doorway between their two offices. A door she had opened without even the courtesy of knocking first.

'Surely there's a coffee-making machine in Lexie's office?'

'I don't drink coffee.'

'There are drinks machines on each floor, and a company restaurant on the eighth floor.' Gideon should have known that the past hour and a half of relative peace and quiet wasn't going to last with Joey McKinley in the building! 'I'm sure you can get hot chocolate there.'

'But not with whipped cream on top, or served by a buff twenty-year-old male with shoulder-length blond hair, I bet.'

Gideon's frown deepened as he thought of the three slightly plump, kindly middle-aged women who usually worked in the restaurant two floors below. 'Well…no.'

'There you go, then.'

'I take it this "buff" vision of manhood *does* work in the coffee shop down the road?'

'Oh, yes.' She smiled at him. 'So, do you want anything? Something to drink? Muffin? Pastry?'

'No, thank you,' he answered, with a barely repressed shudder.

'No to just the drink, or no to all of it?'

Gideon gritted his teeth at her persistence. 'All of it.'

'They do a really great lemon muffin—'

'I said no and I meant *no!*' Gideon was growing more and more irritated. If he wanted coffee he had his own pot, already made on the percolator, and if he wanted something to eat then he would send his secretary—Lucan's secretary, now that Joey McKinley had commandeered his own—down to the restaurant to get it for him.

Joey lingered in the doorway, seemingly unperturbed by his irritability. 'Tell me, Gideon, have you ever been into a coffee shop?'

'No,' he bit out tersely.

'How about a burger place?'

'If by that you are referring to a fast food restaurant, then the answer is no. Neither have I ever been roller skating, hang-gliding or scuba-diving—and I feel no more inclination to do any of them than I do to go to the coffee shop down the street!'

'Nix to the scuba-diving—I've never been too sure what's lurking down there in the depths,' Joey said with a contrived little shudder. 'But I've been roller skating and hang-gliding and loved both of them. As for fast food places and the coffee shop—you have no idea what you're missing!'

'In the case of the coffee shop, apparently a twenty-year-old male with shoulder-length blond hair.' His mouth twisted. 'Who obviously isn't my type. And isn't he a little on the young side for *you*?' he added with disdain.

'Younger men are all the rage at the moment.' Joey McKinley was completely undaunted as she wiggled suggestive auburn brows at him. 'Probably has something to do with the fact that they have more stamina in bed than older guys.'

Gideon stiffened. Who on *earth* had conversations like this one? Joey McKinley, apparently! Personally, he never discussed any of his own brief physical relationships with a third party, and he wasn't enjoying these insights into Joey's private life, either. Especially when she included slights to older men in her blunt commentary. He couldn't help wondering—and he was severely annoyed with himself for doing so—whether she meant men of his own age!

He leant back in his chair to look across at

her from between narrowed lids. 'I would have thought experience would win over stamina every time.'

Joey almost shouted her *yes*! out loud, at having actually managed to engage the aloof Gideon St Claire in this slightly risqué conversation. His whole I-am-an-island thing was like a red rag to a bull as far as she was concerned; she wanted to say outrageous things purely to shock him out of it!

With the weak February sun shining through the huge window behind him Gideon's hair was the colour of pure gold. It looked as if it would be soft and silky to the touch. His eyes were dark and enigmatic between those narrowed lids, and there was a slight smile curving the sensuous line of his lips—as if he were enjoying the conversation in spite of himself.

Joey's hands clenched at her sides as she resisted the urge she felt to cross the office and see if his hair really *would* be soft and silky to the touch. This was Gideon St Claire, she reminded herself impatiently. The man she had believed—*until earlier this morning*, a little voice reminded her—to be completely immune to all emotional feeling.

'Don't knock the stamina until you've tried it,' she said wickedly.

That sensuous mouth thinned immediately. 'Which you obviously have.'

As it happened, no…

Oh, Joey knew she gave off an image of eating up men of all ages for breakfast, and that most people assumed she lived alone and was unmarried through choice. But the truth of the matter was she had been too busy, too single-minded in attaining her law degree during her late teens and early twenties, to have much time left over for relationships. In fact, she'd had no time for them at all. There had been the occasional date, of course—the one with Jason Pickard six months ago being the most recent. And look how successfully *that* had turned out! But she had never been in the sort of long-term and loving relationship she felt necessary, and longed for. Her parents had been happily married for over thirty years, and Joey had decided at a young age that she wasn't going to settle for anything less.

Unfortunately, the downside of the tough,

uncaring image she had deliberately adopted was that it tended to completely overwhelm weak men, and the strong ones just felt threatened by her. Which was probably why, at the age of twenty-eight, abrasive, driven Joey McKinley hadn't yet managed to find a man she could love completely and who loved her in the same way.

And the same reason she was still a virgin...

Something she was sure the cynical Gideon St Claire would find very hard to believe.

'Not yet—but I'll be happy to let you know when I have,' she came back provocatively.

Gideon winced as he sat forward to lean his elbows stiffly on the desktop in front of him. 'Do I take it that there's some sexual connection between the whipped cream and the buff twenty-year-old?'

Those green eyes widened, and for an instant Gideon could have sworn he saw a slight blush to those creamy cheeks. As if the outspoken Joey McKinley was actually *embarrassed* by his comment. He was intrigued at the thought...

'Whew—I think I'm having a hot flush, just thinking about it!' She waved a hand in front of her face.

Gideon sighed. 'If you've quite finished interrupting my morning, I have a business meeting to go to in a few minutes, followed by a luncheon appointment,' he told her.

The provocative smile instantly disappeared, to be replaced by professional interest. 'Do you need me to come with you to either of them?'

Did he need to spend any more time today with this irritating, outspoken and highly disturbing woman? 'No,' he assured her firmly. 'The business meeting isn't going to last long, and the luncheon appointment is personal.'

'Okaaay…' She eyed him speculatively.

'As in none of your business,' he said grimly.

'Fine.' She gave an unconcerned shrug. 'Well, you know where to find me if you need me.'

'Either in the office next door, or at the coffee shop down the road having fantasies about whipped cream and attractive young men, apparently,' Gideon drawled with cool derision.

'Hey, I think you're finally starting to enjoy my sense of humour!' Joey murmured appreciatively.

'Lord, I hope not,' he muttered with feeling.

She gave a husky laugh, before turning to go

back into her own office and closing the door softly behind her.

Gideon drew in a sharp breath. Three weeks, four days, six and a half hours—and counting.

Until Joey McKinley was out of the St Claire Corporation building.

Out of the office next door.

Out of Gideon's life altogether...

CHAPTER THREE

JOEY was still so unsettled by the manner in which Gideon had neatly turned the tables on her with his remark about whipped cream that she completely forgot to ask for any on her hot chocolate—and didn't even notice that it was a young girl serving today, rather than the golden-haired god!

Maybe Gideon really wasn't as uptight as she had always thought him to be if he could make sexual references like that? After all, Stephanie hadn't been able to stop laughing when Joey had asked her if Gideon was gay. Just because Joey had never seen him with a woman it didn't mean Gideon didn't have one in his life—perhaps there was. Just not someone he wanted to take to a family wedding.

To her intense discomfort, just imagining lying naked on a bed with white silk sheets and having the heat of Gideon's tongue lapping whipped cream from her bare breasts was enough to make Joey's nipples go hard inside her bra.

This was *so* not a good idea—

'Get you anything else...?'

Joey looked up blankly at the young girl behind the counter, a blush darkening her cheeks as she realised her hot chocolate was sitting there, ready for her to collect, and there was a queue of people behind her still waiting to be served.

'No. That's fine. Thank you,' she muttered awkwardly as she grabbed up the hot chocolate and made a quick about face, instantly bumping into the bearded man standing directly behind her in the queue. 'Sorry.' She grimaced awkwardly.

'No problem,' he replied.

Joey hurried out of the coffee shop before she did anything else to embarrass herself, breathing deeply once she was outside on the pavement and grateful for the cold February wind to cool her hot and flushed cheeks. She was aware that her hands were trembling slightly as her fingers curled tightly about the warmth of the cup containing the hot chocolate.

What the hell was *wrong* with her? Well... she knew very well what was wrong—she'd been aroused by a sexual fantasy about Gideon St Claire and whipped cream in the middle of a coffee shop! He was the very *last* man Joey should ever think of in that way—especially as they were going to be working closely together for the next four weeks.

Gideon didn't even *like* her, and certainly didn't approve of her, so what on earth—?

'Are you feeling okay?'

Joey looked up to see that the bearded man from the coffee shop had collected his order and was now standing beside her on the pavement. *Was* she feeling okay? Well, she didn't know about that—she was hot, bothered and aroused! Something she hadn't felt for a long time—if ever.

'You're looking a little feverish,' the man continued. 'Perhaps you're coming down with a cold? There's a lot of it about. It's the weather, of course. One day it's cold and the next it's sunny.'

'Yes, probably,' Joey answered awkwardly, looking up at the man for the first time.

He looked to be aged in his late thirties, and was quite handsome from what she could tell through the dark beard that hid most of his lower face. His eyes were a deep and pleasant blue. He also looked vaguely familiar...

'Do I know you?' she asked politely.

'I'm sure I would have remembered you if we had met before.' He gave her a brief, noncommittal smile.

Joey accepted the compliment. 'Sorry to have held you up in there. I was miles away.' On a bed with silk sheets, with Gideon... *No*! She had to stop thinking about that!

'As I said, no problem,' the man assured her lightly. 'Do you work around here?'

Joey frowned slightly; it was one thing to apologise to this man for holding him up, but she wasn't about to tell a complete stranger where she worked. A stranger who still looked vaguely familiar, despite his denial...

'Yes. And it's time I was getting back.' She smiled again, to take the sting out of her dismissal, as she turned to walk away.

'Enjoy your hot chocolate,' he called after her.

'Thanks.' Joey was a little disconcerted to realise that the man must have been aware of her enough earlier to have noticed she had ordered hot chocolate to go. And she was sure she felt his blue eyes following her as she walked back down the street.

Paranoid.

She was becoming paranoid. The man was just being polite to show that he wasn't annoyed at being delayed, for goodness' sake. She was probably just feeling oversensitive after indulging in that steamy fantasy.

Probably? She was *definitely* feeling oversensitive. And in all the wrong places too.

'Good lunch?'

Gideon had only just arrived back in the office, and he drew in a sharp breath as he turned and saw Joey, once again standing in the connecting doorway between their two offices.

'I think we need to lay down a few ground rules, Joey,' he rasped as he removed his jacket and hung it in the closet before moving to sit behind Lucan's imposing desk. 'The first one being that in future I would prefer you to knock before you come barging into my office.'

'Why?'

He clenched his teeth. 'Because I would *prefer* it,' he repeated evenly.

She twinkled at him. 'Are you going to be doing something...*private* in here that you don't want me to walk in on?'

Three weeks, six days, two hours—and counting!

Gideon felt a nerve pulsing in his tightly clenched jaw. 'I just don't like you coming in here unannounced.'

Joey had decided, during the three hours since she had last seen Gideon, that the best way to deal with her earlier lapse into fantasyland was to face it head on. To face *him* head-on.

Looking at him now, as he sat behind Lucan's desk, golden hair slightly ruffled from the cool breeze outside, his jacket removed and the width of his shoulders and muscled chest clearly visible beneath that white silk shirt, suddenly she wasn't so sure...

Oh, get a grip, Joey, she instructed herself impatiently. So she'd had a sexual fantasy about the man? So what? Yes, Gideon was as handsome as sin, but he had just been out for a minimum two-hour lunch with another woman. No doubt a woman only too happy to cater to his sexual preferences, whatever they were…

'My mother sends her regards, by the way.'

Joey blinked. 'Your mother?'

Gideon gave a mocking smile—almost as if he had known exactly what she was thinking. 'I had lunch with her before she caught the afternoon train back to Edinburgh.'

The still beautiful and very gracious Molly St Claire. Dowager Duchess of Stourbridge now, following Lucan's marriage to Lexie on Saturday. And apparently the woman Gideon had just had a two-hour lunch with…

Was that *relief* Joey was feeling? If it was, then it was totally inappropriate. Ridiculous, even, when he had already made it perfectly obvious she was the last woman he would ever be attracted to.

And was she attracted to him?

Well, she was a woman with a pulse and a heartbeat, wasn't she?

Maybe she was—but she wasn't a *stupid* woman with a pulse and a heartbeat! Being attracted to Gideon—a man who showed no interest in her, and no emotion whatsoever for anyone other than those he considered his close family—would be the height of stupidity on her part.

She might choose to present an outer shell of sophistication, but inside Joey knew herself to be as soft as marshmallow—as emotional and vulnerable, in fact, as her outwardly softer twin. She really wasn't about to get her heart broken by falling for the coldly unattainable Gideon St Claire.

'What an attentive son you are, to be sure,' she commented.

Gideon visibly stiffened. 'Maybe you aren't aware of it, but the wedding on Saturday was a difficult time for my mother.'

Joey instantly felt guilty at this reminder that Lucan and Lexie's wedding must have been something of an ordeal for Molly St Claire; Lexie was the granddaughter of Sian Thomas—the woman Molly's husband, Alexander St Claire, the previous Duke of Stourbridge, had left Molly for twenty-five years ago.

Some sort of truce on the past had been called between the two older women before Lucan and Lexie's wedding on Saturday, but even so it couldn't have been an easy time for Gideon's mother.

'I am aware of it.' Joey grimaced in acknowledgement of her faux pas. 'Sorry.'

Gideon continued to eye her coldly for several seconds, before giving an abrupt nod. 'Let's move on, shall we? What did you want to see me about?'

What *did* she want to see Gideon about? Oh, yes. 'Jordan rang while you were out; he and Steph have arrived safely back in LA.'

Gideon nodded. 'He left a message on my voicemail.

It still felt slightly odd to him that he and this woman were connected by the marriage of their twin siblings. Not that he and Jordan were identical twins. But Joey and Stephanie were—even if they chose to be completely different in appearance. Gideon had always thought Stephanie to be warm and charming, while her sister had all the softness of a porcupine. An impression that had been shaken earlier that morning, when he'd heard the aching loneliness in Joey's voice as she'd admitted how much she missed her twin...

Gideon had actually found himself thinking of Joey during lunch, as he and his mother ate dessert. Well, it had been his mother's dessert that had actually triggered the memory—fresh strawberries covered in whipped cream. To his horror and intense discomfort he had found himself imagining Joey lying back on red satin sheets—they would have to be red; he already knew how beautiful her exotic-coloured hair looked against red—while he sensuously licked cream from every inch of her naked body.

The image had been so startlingly vivid that Gideon had felt himself harden, his erection hot and aching beneath the table where he and his mother sat eating together! He'd had to discreetly drape his napkin across his thighs in case anyone noticed that throbbing bulge in his trousers.

'How did your visit to the coffee shop go earlier?' His tone was all the harsher because of his unprecedented reaction to just imagining Joey naked.

There was no way she could have prevented the blush that warmed her cheeks as she was instantly reminded of her drift off into fantasyland earlier. Her breasts became fuller, the nipples hard and sensitive as they chafed against the black lace of her bra.

She moistened dry lips. 'It was—good, thanks.'

Gideon gave her a tight smile. 'Any luck with the buff young god?'

Joey wasn't sure she would have noticed him earlier, even if he *had* been on duty today. Not when her thoughts had been so vividly fixed on Gideon.

Those images of the two of them in bed suddenly flashed into her brain again, so that she couldn't even look him in the face as she answered. 'I'm still working on it.'

Gideon stood up as Joey turned to leave the office, crossing the distance between them in long, purposeful strides. She turned round to face him as he spoke.

'Thank you for passing on the message that Jordan and Stephanie arrived back in LA safely.' His voice was now huskily soft.

'A superfluous message, as it happens,' she commented, very much aware of how close Gideon was now standing to her.

'But you didn't know that,' he said. 'And,

despite my earlier comments, I appreciate you coming to tell me as soon as I returned from lunch.'

Joey smiled. 'Even if I did come *barging* into your office?'

'Even so,' Gideon allowed ruefully, realising how tiny she was as he stood only inches away from her; her manner was always so mocking, so forcefully independent, that she had somehow always seemed...more fiercely substantial to him.

Her admission earlier of missing Stephanie had given Gideon a different insight into her—had hinted at that forceful independence being a defensive veneer rather than an intrinsic part of her nature. Perhaps a defence mechanism that came into play to hide the vulnerability that lay beneath her surface bravado—the same vulnerability that had enabled Joey to sing with such beauty and depth of emotion at Jordan and Stephanie's wedding, maybe?

Joey was shorter than Gideon had thought too. The top of her head only reached up to his chin— no, that couldn't be right. This morning, in the underground car park, he distinctly remembered that her eyes had been level with his mouth as they'd talked.

Gideon stood back slightly to look down at her feet. 'You aren't wearing any shoes...'

Even Joey's feet were beautiful—her ankles shapely, her toes gracefully slender, with pearly pink nails at their tips.

'I have a habit of taking them off whenever I sit down,' Joey admitted.

'It's a little...unorthodox when you're at work.' It also, Gideon realised with a frown, gave an intimacy to this situation that he would rather didn't exist.

She tossed her head. 'Haven't you noticed? I *am* unorthodox!'

Gideon had noticed far too many things about this woman today! Such as the softness of her hair. The creaminess of her skin. The fullness of her breasts beneath the silk of her blouse. The delicious curves of her hips and bottom. The slight vulnerability to those sensuously full lips when she wasn't being smart-mouthed...

Joey was very aware of the sudden tension that surrounded herself and Gideon. She was also aware, so close to him like this, that his chest appeared as hard and muscled as she had imagined it would be, and her senses were being bombarded equally with the heat of his body and his smell: an elusive spicy aftershave mixed with hot and heady male.

She was almost afraid to breathe, and she resisted the impulse she had to step closer to him, to put her arms about his waist and feel the ripple of muscles beneath his shirt as her palms rested against his back. She was certain that he would feel good to touch. Hot and hard. Like steel encased in velvet.

It was a dangerous impulse—especially after the erotic thoughts Joey had had about him earlier on today. And yet she couldn't move away. Could feel the mesmerising pull of his seductive heat. Couldn't take her gaze from those hard and chiselled features. Except they didn't look quite so hard any more. Gideon's mouth was more relaxed than Joey had ever seen it—lips slightly parted, his breath a warm caress against her brow—and his eyes...oh, God, his eyes...

They were no longer just that dark and brooding bitter chocolate brown, but now had shards of gold fanning out from the pupil. That gold deepened, increased as his gaze shifted from her eyes to her parted lips. As if he too were imagining what it would feel like if they were to kiss—

A knock sounded softly on the outer door before it was immediately opened.

'Gideon, I—Oh!'

Lucan's secretary, May Randall, came to an awkward halt in the doorway, her eyes wide as she stared across the room and saw the two of them standing so close together.

'I—I'll come back later!' Her cheeks were bright red as she turned away and shut the door behind her.

May's unexpected interruption had the same effect as a cold shower on Gideon, bringing him instantly to a sense of exactly what he was doing—and what he had been about to do.

Damn it, he had been about to kiss Joey McKinley. *Joey McKinley*, for heaven's sake!

She was everything Gideon disliked in a woman.

The women who briefly held a place in his life were chosen for having the same qualities as his favourite white wine: cool and crisp, with just a hint of seduction to tantalise the senses. Joey had all the explosive qualities of a rich and ruby-red wine: deep and fruity to the palate, with a headiness that attacked rather than tantalised the senses.

Joey only had to take one brief glance up into Gideon's expressive face to know that he regretted even this much of a lapse in the previous antagonism that had existed between them. It was there in the way he breathed deeply through his nose, in his eyes, now a dark glitter, his stiff shoulders, hands tightly clenched at his sides.

Whereas *she* was still reeling from the very real and heart-pounding desire that had ripped through to her very core as she'd become mesmerised by the intensity of emotion burning in the deep gold of his eyes.

Eyes that had suddenly been the same colour as the beloved dragon sitting on her desktop…

CHAPTER FOUR

'AND how do you suggest we explain *that* touching little scene to May?' Gideon barked.

Coldly. Harshly. Disapprovingly. Typically!

The warmth Joey had thought she'd seen as she looked up into the depths of Gideon's gold-coloured eyes had to have been an illusion, she inwardly derided herself as she saw those eyes were now a deep and scathing brown.

'What's to explain?' she dismissed flippantly. 'We were only talking.'

'We were obviously standing much too close to be discussing business contracts.'

Gideon realised with self-disgust that after only a single morning of working with Joey he was already starting to lose his mind. What other explanation could there possibly be for even *thinking* about kissing her? Thinking? He hadn't been thinking at all as he gazed down at her soft and moistly parted lips!

'Personally, I think we're better off just forgetting about it,' Joey said with a shrug. 'It's been my experience that people will carry on thinking what they want about you, no matter what you might have to say on the subject, so it's better not even to bother to offering explanations in the first place.'

Gideon frowned slightly as he heard the underlying thread of cynicism in her voice. Was it because most people—including him—tended to judge her on that let-people-think-of-me-what-they-will attitude? It was an opinion Gideon knew he was guilty of harbouring towards her, and it had already been made something of a nonsense of earlier that morning. And yet it was an opinion he had to continue to maintain if he were to have any defences against the attraction he obviously now felt for her—perhaps always had?

'Maybe you don't care what people think about you, Joey, but I do,' he said coldly. 'Especially people I have to work with on a daily basis.'

Bright wings of angry colour heightened her previously pale cheeks. 'You're working with *me* on a daily basis at the moment, Gideon—perhaps you would be interested to know what *I* think of *you*?'

No, he really didn't care to hear what Joey's opinion of him was!

She had made it obvious from their very first meeting in her office two months ago that she didn't like his high-handed attitude, or him—that in fact, she resented his interference in solving the problem of Stephanie having been wrongly accused of being 'the other woman' in the divorce of Richard Newman, one of her male ex-patients. An accusation Newman, for reasons of his own, had been happy to allow to continue.

Gideon had only stepped in at Jordan's behest, when his brother had become worried about the mental stability of Richard Newman's wife Rosalind, who had come dangerously close to causing Stephanie physical harm in her distress over the divorce. Maybe Gideon *could* have been a little more tactful in the way he had resolved the situation. Maybe he *should* have consulted Joey, who at the time had been acting on Stephanie's behalf, before instructing a private investigator to follow Richard Newman and ascertain who the man was really having an affair with. That it had turned out to be his boss's wife explained the man's reluctance to clear Stephanie of blame!

Gideon hadn't hesitated in using that knowledge to extract Stephanie from all involvement in the divorce, and he hadn't felt any guilt when Richard Newman had deservedly lost his job, as well as his wife and family.

Yes, Gideon accepted that he might have handled the situation more tactfully than he had, by including Joey in what he was doing, but he liked and respected Stephanie, knew how much Jordan loved her, and at the time hadn't thought of how Joey might interpret his behavior. He had only been concerned with extricating her sister from what had rapidly been becoming a dangerous situation.

He realised now—although Joey had obviously been relieved to have her sister removed from that tangled web—she had every reason to resent the arrogance of Gideon's abrupt intervention. The resentment had been there in Joey's manner towards him every time the two of them had spoken since...

He owed this woman an apology, Gideon acknowledged. An apology he daren't even *think* of offering at this moment, when emotions had been so heightened between them a few minutes ago.

'Only if I can return the favour and tell you what I think of you too,' he said.

Perhaps not, Joey acknowledged. Earlier fantasies of being held in Gideon's arms aside, they obviously just didn't like each other.

'I'll pass, thanks,' she replied in a bored voice.

'Then perhaps we should both just get back to work?' He raised dark brows in mute query.

No, they didn't like each other at all!

'Yes, sir!' She gave a mocking salute before turning to go back to her own office.

'Joey?'

She looked back at him with guarded eyes. 'Yes?'

'Put some shoes on, hmm? It sets a bad example for the troops!'

Joey's husky laugh was completely spontaneous, and the shake of her head rueful as she sobered. 'Be careful, Gideon—you might start to develop that sense of humour, after all!'

His mouth twisted wryly. 'I doubt it, when I have that I'm-so-superior stick up my backside.'

She looked ashamed. 'I shouldn't have said that to you.'

Gideon shrugged. 'Why not? If it's what you really think.'

Joey was no longer sure *what* she thought of him. Maybe there were reasons why Gideon was always so emotionally shut-off? An impression that had been severely dented earlier, when he'd admitted that he missed his own twin as much as Joey missed hers, she had to acknowledge.

The break-up of his parents' marriage when Gideon was only ten years old couldn't have been a pleasant experience. Stephanie had confided in her that Alexander St Claire's abandonment of his wife and three sons twenty-five years ago had definitely affected Jordan's opinion of long-term relationships. Perhaps Gideon had similar issues? Maybe that was the reason—

Good Lord—she couldn't actually be making *excuses* for this man's coldness, could she?

'Would you please leave, Joey, and allow me to get on with some work?' he growled, and at the same time pointedly moved to sit behind his desk.

No, Joey answered her own question. She certainly *wasn't* about to make excuses for Gideon; he *was* cold and arrogant and superior, and every other uncomplimentary name she had ever called him—to his face or otherwise!

Gideon watched through narrowed lids as Joey finally left his office, waiting until the door had clicked firmly closed behind her before leaning against the back of his chair to let out a deep sigh.

He was acutely aware that the reason he had moved so quickly to sit behind Lucan's desk was because he was once again aroused by thoughts of passionately kissing Joey McKinley—and he wanted to do more to her than just kiss her, damn it!

Three weeks, six days, and one hour and thirty minutes of this torture left to get through…

'Need any help?'

Joey closed her eyes and wished herself anywhere but down on her knees in the underground car park of the St Claire Corporation, with Gideon looming over her as she attempted to replace the tyre that had gone flat since she'd left her car parked there that morning.

She had left her office a little before six o'clock, convinced by the silence in the adjoining office that Gideon had already left for the day—until she'd arrived in the underground car park and seen their cars were the only two still parked there. Even so, she had still hoped to get away before Gideon came down in the lift.

It was a hope that had been dashed once she had approached her car and found that the front tyre on the driver's side was completely flat. Which was why, after trying to pump the thing up again with no success, Joey was now down on her knees on the blanket she had spread on the oil-spattered concrete, attempting to replace the wheel with the spare from the boot of her car. She'd heard the lift descending and then Gideon walking over to her.

'It's nothing I can't handle,' she assured him as she continued to struggle with that last nut.

'Would you like me to—?'

'No!'

Gideon bit back a smile at Joey's vehemence,

well aware of the reason for it, and knowing that she didn't like appearing at a disadvantage any more than he did. 'Perhaps I could——?'

'Perhaps you could just get into your damned car, drive away and let me get on with this!' she grated as she turned to glare up at him.

Maybe he would have done just that if he'd thought she was ever going to be able to get that wheel off and replace it with the spare. Although perhaps not: one thing Molly St Claire had drummed into her three sons when they were growing up was that a gentleman always helped a lady in distress. And, whether Joey liked it or not, she was definitely in distress.

Besides which, he had no intention of driving away and leaving a woman alone in a deserted car park at almost six-thirty on a dark winter's evening.

'Give that to me,' he instructed firmly as he moved to kneel beside her on the blanket and took the wrench out of her hand. Or at least attempted to take it, because her fingers instantly tightened about the metal tool, refusing to relinquish it.

'Joey, stop being so damned childish and give me the spanner!' Gideon glared down at her.

Jade green eyes glared right back at him. 'I'm not being childish. I just resent being treated like the helpless little woman to your big strong man!'

Gideon growled in his throat. 'Would it help you to know that I consider you as helpless as a Sherman tank?'

Joey's lips twitched at the description coming so soon after his comment earlier about 'the troops'. 'We aren't in a war zone, you know, Gideon.'

'No?' He arched blond brows.

'No.'

'Then stop being so stubbornly independent and give me the spanner.' He met her gaze challengingly.

Joey slowly released the metal tool into his hand, and sat back on her heels to watch as he easily undid that last traitorous nut before sliding the wheel off completely. He stood up to place it in the boot of her car, and then briskly rolled over the spare.

'Don't you just hate it when that happens?' she muttered irritably as she straightened up.

Gideon smiled at her patent annoyance. 'It's no reflection on your capabilities that the last nut was slightly rusted.'

Maybe it wasn't, but Joey *hated* appearing less than capable of dealing with her own problems.

'There didn't seem to be a problem with the tyre this morning…' She strolled over to the boot of her car to inspect it, but couldn't see any visible reason for the puncture. 'Never mind. I'll go and get a replacement at lunchtime tomorrow.' She turned to look over to where Gideon had finished putting on the spare and was now tidying the tools back into the box before folding the blanket.

His tailored suit and white silk shirt were as pristine as always, but there was a small smudge of oil just to the left of his mouth, which meant he probably had oil on his hands, too.

'Here you go.' He placed the toolkit and the folded blanket back in the boot, beside the punctured tyre.

Joey swallowed. 'I—thanks for your help.'

'No problem.'

'Nevertheless, it was kind of you.'

His mouth twisted wryly. 'Considering how ungracious you were when I first offered?'

Joey frowned slightly. 'I don't remember you offering. As usual, you just took over.'

'The way I took over in the Newman case a couple of months ago?'

Joey looked up sharply at the gentleness—and the unexpectedness—of Gideon's query.

'Yes,' she finally answered slowly. 'Exactly the way you took over in the Newman case.'

'I owe you an explanation and an apology for that.'

Joey's uncertainty deepened. Her resentment towards Gideon's arrogant intervention two months ago was the basis upon which she had placed all her future dealings with him. If he now explained and apologised she would have no defences against this rapidly growing attraction she felt towards him. Towards a man who so clearly showed that he only tolerated her at best...

'Joey...?'

Her startled gaze moved up to meet shrewd

brown eyes, and there was a hint of a blush in her cheeks. 'I'm sure you had your reasons for doing it.'

He nodded. 'Because I liked Stephanie from the first, and Jordan asked me to see what I could do to help her. But I realise now that I should have considered your feelings before I acted.'

Much as Joey appreciated knowing that Gideon liked her twin enough to want to help her, she really wasn't sure she could cope right now with his apology. It had been such a strange day already. Not least because she had realised her deepening attraction towards Gideon had already severely battered the defences she usually kept about her emotions.

'You have a smudge of oil beside your mouth,' she said, deliberately changing the subject.

'I do?' Gideon instantly raised a hand and wiped the wrong cheek.

Why did people invariably do that? Joey wondered ruefully. 'Wrong cheek.'

He quirked one brow. 'Maybe you should just do it for me?'

Joey winced inwardly at the thought of touching him so intimately when she was already so completely aware of him. Maybe it would have been better if she hadn't mentioned that smudge of oil at all!

'I have some wipes in my handbag.' She hurried to open the car door, and bent down to get the wipes from where she had placed her handbag on the passenger seat before attempting to change the wheel, sincerely hoping that the visible warmth in her cheeks would fade by the time she straightened.

'Here.' She held the wipe out to him.

'It really would be easier if you did it for me,' he insisted.

Not for Joey!

'You're a big boy now, Gideon, and perfectly capable of cleaning your own face,' she muttered irritably, her nerves already frayed enough without the added possibility of touching him accidentally. 'Use one of the side mirrors on my car,' she suggested when he didn't move.

Gideon could see Joey's reflection in the mirror as she stood just behind him, and was very aware that not only had she refused to discuss the Newman case with him, but she had also dismissed his attempt at an apology.

Which didn't bode well for them having to continue to work together for the next four weeks...

Gideon's mouth tightened determinedly as he balled the damp wipe into his hand before turning back to face her. 'Look, Joey, we seem to have got off to something of a shaky start—' he began.

'We did that a couple of months ago.'

'And I have just tried to apologise for that,' Gideon reminded her gently. 'Why don't we go somewhere and have a glass of wine together and discuss it further?'

Much as he might have thought he was acting for the best at the time, he knew that if the situations had been reversed he would have felt exactly the same resentment she did.

Joey didn't want to 'go somewhere' and have *anything* with Gideon St Claire! Not if it meant she would be in danger of the physical attraction that had been growing between them throughout the day deepening even further.

Something had changed, she realised—shifted in their opinions of each other. And it was a shift Joey wasn't altogether comfortable with.

Verbally sparring with Gideon was one thing, feeling anything else for a man who totally rejected having any of the softer emotions in his life was something else completely.

Besides which, she wasn't one hundred per cent sure his offer wasn't because he felt sorry for her after her admission earlier of missing Stephanie.

'I have plenty of friends I can share a glass of wine with if I feel in need of company, thank you, Gideon. In fact—' she gave a pointed glance at her wristwatch '—I have a date this evening, so I really need to get going if I want to make it on time.'

Gideon's mouth thinned. 'With Jason Pickard?'

'As it happens, yes. Do you have a problem with that?' She met the darkness of his gaze head-on.

'Not in the least,' Gideon denied, obviously regretting whatever impulse had made him make the offer in the first place. 'I hope the two of you have a nice evening.'

'Oh, I'm sure that we will,' Joey taunted. 'Jason is wonderful company.'

When he wasn't in a fluster, that was, because

he and Trevor had had yet another argument—usually over the fact that Jason still hadn't told his parents about the two of them!

'No doubt,' Gideon drawled, with a marked lack of interest. 'You probably shouldn't wait until lunchtime to get your tyre replaced tomorrow, so I'll understand it if you're a little late in the morning.'

'Is that a suggestion or an order?' Joey raised mocking brows.

His eyes narrowed. 'I believe it's I'll understand if you're a few minutes late coming in tomorrow morning. You might have to wait until the garage opens so you can get your tyre replaced.'

Strange how Gideon's so-called 'understanding' sounded just like an order...

Or maybe Joey really was just over-sensitive where this particular man was concerned? If anyone else had made the same offer she would have believed they were being kind. Kindness just wasn't an emotion Joey associated with the icily reserved Gideon St Claire.

However, he *had* admitted that it was his liking of Stephanie and his love for Jordan that had prompted his arrogant interference in the

Newman case. And he had also demonstrated today that he had a sense of humour, after all. Just as the way his eyes had changed from dark brown to gold earlier had been demonstrative of another emotion. Joey just wasn't sure quite what that emotion had been...

'In that case I'll do as you suggest. Thank you,' she added gruffly.

'You're welcome,' Gideon said, aware of how much that 'thank you' had cost her.

Perhaps it was as well Joey had refused his invitation; spending part of his evening in a verbal slanging match with her as he futilely tried to explain the reasons for his interference two months ago was *not* what Gideon would consider a pleasant way of spending his precious spare time.

He had no idea what his plans were for the evening. Being with his family over the weekend—his twin, especially—had left Gideon feeling restless now they had all returned to their respective homes.

Maybe he would just spend a quiet evening at home in his apartment? Or perhaps he should give Valerie Temple a call; she had seemed receptive to a dinner invitation from him when they had met at an art exhibition a couple of weeks ago.

Whatever he decided to do, Gideon couldn't help but take note of the fact that Joey had refused his invitation because she had a date with the man she had earlier told him she wasn't romantically involved with, and he was infuriated with his own interest in the matter.

'Enjoy your evening,' he muttered as he turned away.

'You too,' Joey murmured distractedly as she watched Gideon walk over to his own car.

Surely that wasn't *disappointment* she was feeling because he hadn't insisted that surely she had time to join him for one glass of wine, at least, before her date with Jason?

It couldn't be!

Could it…?

CHAPTER FIVE

'WOULD you happen to know anything about the air being let out of two of the tyres on my car?'

Joey looked up in amazement as Gideon burst unannounced into her office late on Wednesday evening, a coldly accusing expression on his face as he spat the question at her.

The last couple of days working at the St Claire Corporation had passed in much the same way as the first one had. Well, without Joey meeting Gideon first thing in the morning in the car park. Or any conversation about the buff young man in the coffee shop. Or the verbal sparring. Oh, and without Gideon inviting her to join him for a glass of wine after work because he wanted to explain and apologise to her for his behaviour two months ago...

Apart from those things, Tuesday and Wednesday had been pretty much like Monday!

In actual fact, Joey had hardly seen Gideon

these past forty-eight hours. His car was already parked in his spot in the car park when she arrived in the mornings, and any work he had for her had either arrived mysteriously on her desk by the time she came in, or was delivered by May Randall later in the morning.

The connecting door between their two offices had remained firmly closed. Gideon obviously felt no necessity to talk to her, and Joey was experiencing an uncharacteristic reluctance to engage in another bout of verbal sparring with him.

Now this…

'What do you mean?' she asked incredulously.

'Stop playing the innocent, Joey.' Gideon began to pace the office restlessly. 'I should have guessed this past two days of relative peace and quiet were just the calm before the storm. You've just been biding your time, haven't you?' He gave Joey no opportunity to reply before continuing. 'Lulling me into a false sense of security before hitting out!'

'I have absolutely no idea what you're talking about, Gideon,' Joey informed him stiltedly as she stood up slowly. So much for the peace and quiet! 'Why on earth would you assume that *I* had let down the tyres on your car?'

'Who the hell knows how your mind works?' he asked, throwing his hands up into the air. 'Maybe because I openly showed my aversion to allowing you to work here in the first place—'

'Let's get one thing clear, Gideon—*you* didn't *allow* me to do anything,' Joey cut in forcefully, her eyes flashing a warning. 'As I've already told you, my arrangement is with Lucan—and has absolutely nothing to do with you. Your own feelings in the matter are of absolutely no interest to me,' she added scathingly.

'I advise you *make* them of interest,' he advised coldly.

'I don't care to,' Joey snapped.

'Oh, but you *do* care,' Gideon said silkily. 'You obviously care very much.'

Joey blinked, a shutter coming down over her emotions as she wondered if she could in some way have revealed her growing physical attraction to this man. Although how and when she could have done that, considering she hadn't even seen Gideon for the past two days, she had no idea!

'Care about *you*? I don't think so!' she scorned.

'Of course not about me personally.' Gideon dismissed the idea impatiently, making her breathe an inward sigh of relief. 'But no matter how you may have dismissed the idea on Monday I believe you care very much about the fact that I should have consulted with you over the Newman case. And you also feel that once I became aware of what Newman was up to I should have informed you and left you to handle the problem, rather than stepping in and dealing with it myself.'

Joey gave a terse inclination of her head. 'Of course I care about that. If for no other reason than that you should have done both those things out of professional courtesy, if nothing else!'

'I tried to explain and apologise on Monday—'

'Two months later!' Her voice rose. She was very aware that it was the sexual tension that had been slowly building inside her over the past two days that was responsible for her shrewishness now, as much as anything else. 'The fact that you didn't so much as consider my feelings at the time is indicative of how your own inability to feel emotion makes you blind to how another person is feeling.'

'What exactly do you mean by that?' he asked, dangerously calm.

'Oh, come on, Gideon,' Joey said with a short laugh. 'We both know that if your ability to show emotion was compared to that of an iceberg, the iceberg would win every time!'

Gideon looked at Joey from between lowered lids, noting the softness of her red hair. The blouse she was wearing today was of a shimmering red that brought out the blonde and cinnamon highlights in those short tresses and her breasts were a full and tantalising swell beneath that silky material. As for the way her black knee-length skirt moulded to the curve of her hips and perfect bottom... Well, what would she have to say about his lack of emotion if she were to realise how many times just thinking about her these past few days had caused his body to harden and throb?

Just as he was hard and throbbing now...

His eyes narrowed to golden slits as he slowly

walked towards her. 'That's really what you think of me? That I'm incapable of feeling emotion?'

Joey took several steps back as Gideon suddenly became the stalking predator once again—with her as the prey. And she realised—too late—that it was his rigid control over his emotions that made him appear cold, rather than any lack of them. He was no longer making any effort to hide his emotions now, as the focus of his anger and desire became centred on her.

She came to an abrupt halt as she felt the window behind her and realised she had backed as far as she could go. She was now trapped between the coldness of the window and the heat of Gideon's body as he came to a halt mere inches away from her.

Joey licked her lips nervously. 'Maybe I was being a little hasty when I made such a sweeping statement—'

'Maybe?' he drawled softly, that golden gaze holding hers captive as he took that last step which brought his body flush up against hers.

Oh, dear Lord!

Her breath caught in her throat as the heat of Gideon's muscled chest against her breasts caused her nipples to swell to a hot and throbbing ache. Her eyes widened as that throb was echoed between her thighs as he slowly and deliberately pressed the pulsing length of his arousal into her welcoming warmth.

'Still think I lack emotion?' Gideon asked huskily, enjoying flaunting the evidence of his own desire and watching her eyes widen even further.

He captured both of her hands in one of his before raising them above her head and pressing them against the window. At the same time his other hand moved to the buttons on her blouse.

'I— What are you doing?' Joey cursed the mouse-like squeak that was her own voice at the same time as congratulating herself on being able to speak at all. Gideon was unfastening the buttons on her blouse, one slow button at a time, until it was completely undone and he could push the two sides of the material aside to reveal her breasts cupped in black lace.

'I would have thought that was obvious,' Gideon mocked softly, and he deliberately held Joey's startled gaze with his own before that gaze lowered to the swell of her breasts, the dusky-rose of her hardened nipples easily discernible beneath the fine black lace of her bra.

'I— Well— Yes— But—'

'No buts, Joey,' he said gruffly, and he finally lowered his head to taste the creamy length of her throat with his lips, his tongue lingering on the pulsing heat of the blood thrumming just beneath the surface of her creamy skin.

Joey couldn't think when Gideon's body was pressed so intimately against hers—when she could feel the hard pulsing of his considerable erection pressing against the throbbing nubbin nestled between her own thighs.

She groaned low in her throat as his mouth travelled down to the swell of her breasts. The warmth of his hand was moving beneath her loosened blouse to rest against the bareness of her back as he pulled her against him. His tongue stroked a caress against her flesh in a trail across the flimsy black lace to first encircle and then draw one swollen nipple deep into the heat of his mouth.

Joey's knees buckled at the intensity of the pleasure that claimed her as Gideon continued to draw rhythmically on that highly sensitive peak. His tongue swept moistly over that aching nipple again and again, and the place between her thighs pulsed in that same aching rhythm.

Joey desperately sought relief for that ache, parting her legs and allowing herself to press the aroused nubbin between her thighs against the iron-hardness of Gideon's arousal. Her breath was coming in panting sobs as she felt a climax building, growing deep inside her, clamouring for release.

Gideon had only intended to show Joey how wrong she was when she'd accused him of lacking in emotion. But his demonstration had quickly turned to something else—something more basic, primal—and Gideon knew that he wanted this pleasure to continue. *Needed*, to see Joey as she came apart in his arms as orgasm claimed her.

And where did they go from here? a tiny voice of reason mocked deep inside his head. What happened *after* Joey had climaxed? Did he then strip away all their clothes—first from her body and then his own—before draping her over the desk and burying himself to the hilt between her thighs?

Much as might want to do that, Gideon knew that he couldn't. He had already allowed this to go so much further than he had intended. He was more aroused, his body positively aching for release, just from kissing and caressing Joey than when fully making love to another woman. Somehow she stripped away all of his defences and left him feeling vulnerable in a way he had never felt before.

And he certainly didn't want to feel it with Joey McKinley!

Joey felt disorientated, bereft, when Gideon suddenly pulled away from her, leaving desire still coursing hotly through her body. That desire turned swiftly to dismay, and then humiliation, as Gideon looked down at her briefly with dark, enigmatic eyes before turning abruptly on his heel and walking away from her, crossing to the other side of the office to stand with his back towards her.

The other side of Lexie St Claire's office, Joey acknowledged, her embarrassment total as she realised what she had just allowed to happen. How much more could have happened in this public place if Gideon hadn't called a halt to their lovemaking…?

She quickly grasped the two sides of her blouse together over her semi-nakedness, her cheeks blazing with humiliation as she began to refasten the buttons with fingers that trembled and fumbled over the simple task.

Joey knew exactly why Gideon had behaved in the way he had, of course: he had wanted to teach her a lesson for what he had taken as a slight on his emotions. But how could she have let things go as far as they had? *Why* had she? With Gideon St Claire, of all people!

'Point proved, I believe?'

Joey looked up sharply at Gideon's comment, relieved that at least her blouse was once again fastened when she saw that he had turned back to face her, his dark gaze now sweeping over her with what looked like mockery. The fact that she deserved it after responding to him in such an uninhibited way brought the bile rising to the back of Joey's throat—so much so that she had to swallow before answering.

'We've established that you're capable of a physical reaction, at least—if that's what you mean?' She silently congratulated herself for managing to meet the challenge in that dark gaze.

Gideon couldn't help but admire Joey's quick recovery from what had been a dangerous situation for both of them. A danger he was still fully aware of as he looked at the flushed beauty of her face and recalled how much he had enjoyed the taste of her in his mouth.

His mouth tightened as he fought against those memories. 'And so, obviously, are you.'

Colour blazed once again in Joey's cheeks. 'I don't think *my* emotions were ever in question!'

'Well, not any more, no,' Gideon drawled, accepting he was behaving badly, but aware that he needed to re-establish distance between them. Fast! 'Unfortunately none of that provides us with any answers as to how two of the tyres on my car appear to have gone flat at the same time,' he reminded her.

Jade green eyes glittered with anger once again. 'I've already told you I don't know anything about that.'

Yes—and Gideon believed her. Hell, he had

believed her the first time she'd denied it, and had no idea what he'd been doing in the first place, even suggesting that Joey might have done it.

Just being around her on a day-to-day basis was totally screwing with his normal ability for rational thinking, Gideon acknowledged heavily. Even when he avoided her—as he had been trying to do for the past two days—he was still totally aware of her. So much so that it had been all too easy, when he'd left the office and arrived down in the car park to find two of the tyres on his car flat, to apportion the blame to Joey. Impulsively. Irrationally. Gideon was acting completely out of character, and he knew it. He had to pull himself together!

He nodded. 'I'm inclined to believe you—'

'How kind of you,' she shot back sarcastically.

Gideon ignored her. 'I'm also wondering,' he continued, 'whether this and the flat tyre on your own car on Monday night aren't somehow connected.'

Joey stilled. Initially she had been relieved to have the subject changed to something other than

the embarrassment of the intimacies she had allowed Gideon, but with the mention of her own
problem with her car, her attention became fully
engaged on the subject.

'What exactly are you suggesting?'

Gideon shrugged. 'Could you try very hard
not to take it as yet another character defect on
my part when I tell you that I don't believe in
coincidences?'

Neither did Joey. And what were the chances
of two people who worked in the same building
and parked their car in the same car park finding
both their cars had flat tyres within a couple of
days of each other?

'Has anyone else working here had a similar
problem?'

'Not that I'm aware of—and I can do without
any comment from you on how unlikely it is,
with the superior stick-up-my-backside attitude
you say I have, that any of St Claire's employees
would bother to inform me if they *did* have a
problem,' Gideon warned as he saw the sceptical look that had entered those jade-green eyes
at his first comment.

He was aware that she had become popular

with the other members of the staff over the past three days. His own secretary was full of praise for her, as was May Randall. It seemed that he was the only one who had a problem being around her on a daily basis.

'Just accept that I would have heard if there was anything to hear.'

'Okay.' She shrugged. 'Maybe it is just a coincidence, after all?'

'I doubt it.' Gideon grimaced. 'Did the people at the garage give a reason for why your own tyre went flat when you took it in to be repaired yesterday morning?'

'They didn't bother to look,' Joey revealed reluctantly. 'I had all four tyres replaced after the mechanic took one look at them and decided that they wouldn't pass a safety check—I've been busy, okay?' she defended herself when Gideon raised disapproving brows. Could she help it if she was one of those drivers who knew absolutely nothing about the mechanics of her car and only required that it start when she turned the key in the ignition? 'I doubt that there's any way we can check, either. By now all four tyres have probably been consigned to a tyre graveyard.'

'No doubt,' Gideon agreed.

Joey gave a puzzled shake of her head. 'Why just sabotage the two of us, do you think?'

'It's only supposition so far—'

'This isn't a court of law, Gideon,' she jeered gently. 'I promise not to write down anything you say and use it in evidence against you!'

'Very funny,' he drawled dryly.

Not really. But Joey was most comfortable around this man when she was mocking him for one reason or another—she certainly didn't want to think any more just now about the way he had unbuttoned her blouse a few minutes ago and kissed her breasts with a skill and passion that had blown her away.

'There's plenty more where that came from,' she murmured.

'I'm sure there is.' Gideon sighed. 'But it isn't exactly helping us to solve this puzzle, is it?'

'Maybe it was just vandals.' Joey shrugged. 'Kids who are bored and looking for mischief?'

'Maybe,' he said, not looking particularly convinced. 'But I think it should be looked into further before we totally dismiss it as such.'

'And how do you suggest we do that?'

Gideon's gaze sharpened. 'I wasn't suggesting *we* do it at all.'

Joey's eyes widened. 'I hope this isn't going to be another case of the big strong man protecting the helpless little woman?'

'Flattered as I am that you should even *think* of me as a "big strong man", Joey,' Gideon said, noting the wings of colour that appeared in her cheeks at his teasing, 'your own role as helpless little woman is, as usual, seriously in question!'

'Good,' Joey muttered with vehemence—at the same time knowing that helpless was precisely how she had felt a few minutes ago, with her hands raised above her head, her blouse unbuttoned and her breasts being plundered by Gideon's marauding lips and tongue. And she'd loved every second of it!

Looking at him now, every inch his usual cold and aloof self, Joey found it extremely difficult to imagine those intimacies had ever taken place...

'So, how do you suggest *we* proceed?' she pressed on.

'I don't want you involved, Joey,' he insisted.

'Isn't it a little late for that?'

'Involved any further than you already are,' Gideon amended. 'The most sensible thing for you to do is to go home and leave me here to investigate further,' he added grimly.

He had no idea what the hell was going on, and until he did he would feel happier if Joey was safely at home.

She quirked auburn brows. 'No date tonight?'

No date for some time, as it happened. 'No,' he admitted. 'You?'

'No.'

'I hope your agreement to work here for a month isn't in any way affecting your...*friendship* with Jason Pickard?'

As it happened, Jason had finally told his parents the truth about himself and Trevor. The senior Pickards hadn't been overjoyed at the news—especially as they'd realised it meant they would probably never have any grandchildren—but according to Jason they were slowly getting used to the idea.

Which, of course, meant there was no longer any reason for Joey to go out to dinner with Jason...

'Wouldn't it be more sensible if I hung around for a while and helped you to investigate?' Joey said brightly. 'That way I could give you a lift home once we've finished.'

'Not necessary,' Gideon said. 'I've already telephoned my garage, and they're driving over a replacement car and will take mine away to fix it,' he added firmly as Joey would have interrupted again.

Must be nice, Joey acknowledged ruefully; the most the garage who serviced *her* car ever gave her was a bill! Not that they were even open at six-thirty on a Wednesday evening. There were obviously benefits to being Gideon St Claire— *Lord* Gideon St Claire! 'I could still stay and help—'

'Joey, I may have suggested that you're far from being helpless,' he rasped, 'but that doesn't mean I don't still intend to protect you. From yourself, if necessary.'

'You really are a male chauvinist, aren't you?' Joey accused.

He smiled slightly. 'Didn't you miss *pig* out of that statement?'

'Oink!' she muttered, with feeling.

Gideon had to bite back another smile. At the same time he wondered how it was that Joey could so easily turn his mood to amusement as well as anger. Along with several other emotions he would rather not think about right now. Such as an uneasy jealousy of any *friendship* she might have with a certain Jason Pickard...

'Just go home, hmm, Joey,' he said, suddenly deadly serious again.

Her chin rose in direct challenge. 'And what exactly are you going to be doing to investigate after I've gone?'

He gave a noncommittal shrug. 'Checking into a few things.'

'Such as?'

'How about I discuss that with you in the morning?'

Joey eyed him warily, not sure she altogether trusted him to do that, and yet not seeing any hint of evasion in the steadiness of his darkened gaze as it so easily met hers.

Those same eyes had turned the colour of molten gold when he'd looked down at her semi-naked breasts only minutes ago. Well, at least she now had the answer to *that* particular question; Gideon's eyes blazed that beautiful colour when he was aroused—to passion as well as to anger!

Something Joey would probably be better off not thinking about just now...

'Okay.' She gave a stiff nod of her head. 'But I'll expect a full report from you first thing in the morning,' she warned.

'Yes, ma'am!' Gideon echoed her mocking salute of two days ago.

It was somehow an intimately shared gesture that made Joey feel uneasy as she turned away quickly to collect her coat from the back of her chair, keeping her back turned firmly towards Gideon as she thrust her arms into the sleeves of her jacket before straightening her blouse over the collar.

She had accused him of lacking in emotion, but at the same time she knew she had never felt this seesawing of her own emotions until she'd met him. Aroused one minute. Amused the next. With both those emotions usually followed by anger. This uneasiness was new, though...

Her expression was deliberately bland when she

turned back to face him. 'I'll wish you good-night, then.'

''Night.'

Joey gave him one last frowning glance, before picking up her bag and turning to leave, anxious to get away now. Away from the memories of being in his arms…

'And, Joey…?'

She tensed warily, schooling her features into mild curiosity as she looked back over her shoulder at him. 'Yes?'

His face was harsh: eyes glacial, cheekbones defined, jaw clenched. 'I apologise for what happened earlier.'

This wasn't happening. It really *wasn't* happening!

Wasn't it humiliating enough that they both still had the memories of those shared intimacies without Gideon actually apologising for them? That she had to try and work in the office where it had happened for the next three and a half weeks? With the added knowledge that Gideon was in the office next door?

He shook his head. 'It was ridiculous of me to accuse you of vandalising my car.'

Joey's breath left her in a controlled—
relieved!—sigh; he wasn't apologising for kissing and caressing her, after all...

'Forget it, Gideon,' she said pertly. 'After all,
you can't help being a bigoted idiot!'

Gideon found himself chuckling in spite of
himself. No one—absolutely no one—spoke to
him with the same irreverence Joey did. 'You
know, one day you might actually say something
nice about me,' he said wryly.

'You think?'

'I can dream, can't I?'

'I shouldn't hold your breath if I were you!'

Those green eyes openly laughed at him for
several seconds, beguiling him into sharing her
amusement, before she turned and left the office,
flashing him one last triumphant smile on the
way out.

Gideon moved to sit on the side of the desk,
an amused smile still curving his lips. Joey
McKinley was every bit as impossible as he had
always thought her to be.

She was also every bit as desirable as he had
imagined she might be.

Gideon's smiled faded as he thought of those

few intensely pleasurable minutes of making love to Joey. It had been like holding a living flame in his arms. Sensuously seductive. Fiercely hot. With the real possibility of that flame bursting dangerously out of control and consuming him.

Joey herself was every bit as unpredictable, as volatile, as that flame. In fact, he thought uncomfortably, she was every uncertain, unpredictable emotion that he had been at such pains to banish from his own well-ordered life for the past twenty-five years...

CHAPTER SIX

'GIDEON?' To say that Joey was surprised to answer the door of her apartment at almost nine o'clock that evening and find Gideon standing outside had to be an understatement!

It was a less formal Gideon than she was used to seeing, in a thin black cashmere sweater that moulded to his muscled chest and the flatness of his stomach, over a pair of tailored black trousers. The gold of his hair contrasted dramatically with the black clothing, giving him the appearance of a devastatingly handsome fallen angel, and his appearance rendered Joey completely speechless for several seconds.

He shouldn't have come here, Gideon realised when he saw the shocked wariness on Joey's face, before that emotion was quickly replaced by frowning confusion.

'What are you doing here?' Joey prompted, fingers tightly gripping the edge of the door.

As if she were prepared to slam that door in his face if his answer wasn't one that she liked!

No, he really shouldn't have come here, Gideon acknowledged as he saw the wariness return once again to those expressive jade-green eyes. Eyes the same colour as the fitted sweater Joey wore over figure-hugging, low-riding blue jeans. Her face was bare of the make-up she wore during the day, making her look much younger than twenty-eight.

Gideon's mouth twisted. 'Obviously visiting you.'

She chewed briefly on her top lip before answering him. 'How did you even know where I live?'

He shrugged. 'I looked it up in your file.'

Joey's brows rose. 'I have a *file*?'

'Every employee at St Claire's has a file,' he answered dryly. 'Even the ones only employed by us for four weeks.'

'Oh.'

'You don't have any shoes on again...' He looked down at those graceful bare feet, poking out from beneath the bottoms of her jeans.

She shrugged. 'I prefer not to wear them whenever possible.'

He nodded.

'Gideon, why are you here?' she asked again.

Gideon grimaced. 'This was a bad idea, wasn't it?'

Her tongue flicked nervously over her bottom lip. 'That depends...'

His eyes narrowed. 'On what?'

'On what you came here for,' Joey said slowly; it was one thing to deliberately provoke and argue with Gideon in the office, where they were on neutral ground, and something else entirely for him to come to her home like this. Especially after the intimacies they had shared earlier.

If Gideon had come here expecting to carry on where they'd left off, though, he was going to be disappointed. Haunted as Joey might be by those memories, she had no intention of reliving them. No matter how much just seeing him again made her ache to do just that.

It was all too easy for Gideon to see what direction Joey's thoughts had taken. To guess from the sudden warm flush that appeared in her cheeks, followed by the glitter of determination in her eyes, that she was thinking of how he had kissed her and touched her.

Those same thoughts had kept Gideon in a state of increasingly aching arousal for the past three hours!

Was it that which was the real driving force behind his decision to come to Joey's apartment this evening? Oh, he had told himself that his only reason for coming here was so that they could discuss privately whatever was going on with the vandalism to both their cars—he was more convinced than ever that the two incidences were connected. But seeing Joey again now, and becoming increasingly aware of the jealousy he felt just thinking of her friendship with Jason Pickard, he wasn't so sure any more that his motives had been that innocent…

He straightened determinedly. 'I'm here to discuss the fact that the mechanics who came to pick up my car checked the punctures before loading the car onto the trailer, and found that a knife, or something similarly sharp, had been used to slash the inside of the tyres.'

Joey's eyes widened in alarm. 'It was deliberate, then?'

Gideon's expression was grim. 'Undoubtedly.'

She gave another moistening sweep of her tongue across her lips. 'And my own car?'

'The same, probably. After you left earlier I decided to look at the security camera film from the underground car park for today. I couldn't see anything unusual, so I had Security make copies onto disks, and thought we could save some time if we looked through them this evening. You might spot something—or someone— that I missed.' Gideon held up the disks he had brought with him. 'You said earlier that you weren't going out this evening, so I thought—' He stopped and shook his head. 'I shouldn't have come here. This can wait.'

'No! No, it's fine. Come in. Please.' Joey opened the door wider, knowing she was behaving like a nervous virgin by keeping him standing on the doorstep in this way.

Well…she *was* a nervous virgin. But that didn't mean she had to behave like one—especially in front of the obviously experienced Gideon St Claire!

'I was only watching a boring detective pro-gramme on TV, anyway.' Joey closed the door behind Gideon to follow him through to the sit-ting room, switching the television off before turning back to face him. 'Can I get you tea or coffee before we start—er—before we look at the disks?' Damn it—now she was blushing like a nervous virgin, too!

Gideon arched curious brows. 'I thought you didn't drink coffee?'

Joey gave a graceful shrug. 'I don't, but that doesn't mean I don't have some to give to my guests.' She could also do with a few minutes on her own while she made that coffee—if only to allow time for the blush to fade from her cheeks! 'Have you eaten, or can I get you something...?'

'You can cook too?'

'Not really.' She grinned unapologetically. 'Stephanie is the cook in our family. I was really only offering to get you some toast, or some-thing simple like that, if you hadn't eaten dinner yet.'

Gideon gave a rueful smile. 'Just coffee would be great, thanks.'

He lowered his lids guardedly as he watched Joey go through to the kitchen, enjoying looking at the way her gently rounded bottom swayed from side to side in unknowing provocation, before he turned to look at the sitting room in which he stood.

He had somehow expected her apartment to be as crisp and modern as the woman was herself, with art and furniture that tended to be fashionable rather than comfortable. Instead Gideon found himself in a room predominantly in warm autumnal colours: yellow-painted walls, sofa and chairs in a reddish terracotta, with scatter cushions in a mixture of yellows and oranges, and rugs of equally bright colours on the polished wooden floor. The prints on the walls were also unexpected—poppy fields, and ladies in long floaty dresses wandering around abundantly floral gardens.

Could it be that the abrasive and prickly Joey McKinley was secretly a closet romantic?

Joey wasn't sure she liked the look of thoughtful speculation on Gideon's face when she returned from the kitchen, carrying a tray with the coffee and teapots and two cups, a jug of milk and another of cream, and a bowl of sugar.

'You can sit down, you know,' she invited as she placed the tray down on a low coffee table, before sitting down in the middle of the three-seater sofa—a definite hint to Gideon that she expected him to sit in one of the two armchairs.

The few minutes she had spent in the kitchen making coffee and tea hadn't succeeded in dampening her complete physical awareness of him, but she did at least have it under control enough not to give in to the temptation he represented. She hoped!

Gideon hesitated. 'Are you sure I'm not inconveniencing you?'

'Even if you are, you're going to drink this coffee now that I've made it,' she came back tartly as she poured the aromatic brew into one of the cups.

The apartment might be something of a surprise to Gideon, but it was reassuring to know that Joey's manner could be just as acerbic here as it was at the office!

'Black, thanks,' he accepted, and he took the cup of coffee from her before sitting down in the armchair beside the warm gas fire. 'Have you lived here long?'

She shrugged as she sat back on the sofa to drink her tea. 'A couple of years.'

'Have you always lived in London?'

'Steph and I shared a small flat here when we were both at university.'

'Where you studied law?'

'Obviously.'

'Has your singing voice been professionally trained?' Gideon at last voiced the question that had been intriguing him ever since he had heard her sing so angelically at Stephanie and Jordan's wedding.

'Yes.' The answer almost seemed to be forced out of her.

'I had no idea you had such a fantastic voice until I heard you sing at the wedding.'

'That was a special occasion,' she dismissed stiffly.

'Did you never think of—?'

'Gideon, did you come here to ask me a lot of personal questions, or so that we could view the disks?' Joey cut in sharply.

Gideon eyed her quizzically as he sipped his

coffee. 'I was merely curious as to why you didn't pursue a professional singing career.'

'Maybe my voice isn't good enough,' she suggested dryly.

'We both know that it is.'

'It's personal, okay?' Joey said curtly.

'You don't like to talk about yourself, do you?'

'Said the pot to the kettle!'

Gideon smiled. 'You already know that I have a twin, and another brother two years older. My mother lives in Edinburgh—'

'None of those things are just about *you*—they are equally true of Jordan,' Joey pointed out.

'True.' Gideon nodded. 'This is good coffee, by the way.' He took another sip of the strong brew.

'It's also a good diversionary tactic from talking about yourself.' Joey eyed him mockingly.

'Said the kettle to the pot?' he returned, with a definite glint in his eye.

Joey shrugged. 'I guess we both value our privacy.'

Gideon frowned slightly. 'And I've invaded

yours by coming here unexpectedly this evening, haven't I?'

'Stop worrying about it, Gideon. I can always check your own file for your home address and reciprocate one evening!'

Gideon immediately found himself wondering what Joey would make of his own apartment, which, for all it was expensively furnished and decorated, was of a modern and clinical style rather than being casually comfortable. He knew instinctively that she would absolutely hate it.

Which was of absolutely no relevance when he had no intention of ever allowing her to visit him there; his apartment was his personal space, and he only ever invited his close family.

'Perhaps you're right. We should look at the disks now,' he suggested as he leant forward to place his empty cup back on the tray.

'Fine,' Joey answered lightly, easily able to tell that she had unknowingly touched upon a sensitive subject.

Not that she had ever intended visiting him at his place uninvited, but Gideon's adverse reaction was intriguing, nonetheless. Perhaps because he wasn't always alone there, and an unexpected visit from her might prove embarrassing for all of them?

Or it could just be because Gideon valued his privacy even more than she did?

Whatever the reason, his reluctance to have her anywhere near his apartment was more than obvious! As obvious as her own aversion to discussing why, when she acknowledged her voice had been trained, she hadn't pursued a professional singing career...

'Hand me the disks.' Joey stood up to take them from him, crossing the room to where her DVD player was and kneeling down to switch it and the television back on before loading the first disk.

'The cameras are movement-activated, so it isn't as bad as it looks,' Gideon told her after they had watched the first disk showing many of the St Claire employees arriving to park their cars in the morning.

'Perhaps that's as well!' Joey eyed the three discs left to play.

It took almost two hours, and the emptying of both the coffee and the tea pot, before they had viewed all four disks. Like Gideon earlier, Joey had seen nothing unusual on any of them.

Even though she had only worked at St Claire's for three days, she already recognised many of the employees arriving and leaving the building. All very interesting—not!—and not in the least helpful in terms of discovering if anyone had actually tampered with Gideon's car.

'Nothing?' he prompted as the last disk came to an end.

'I'm afraid not.' Joey sighed as she handed all four disks back to him.

'It was a bit of a long shot, anyway,' he acknowledged.

Joey stood up. 'Would you like some fresh coffee?'

'It's getting late. Don't you want to get to bed—' Gideon broke off abruptly as he saw the telling blush that had entered Joey's cheeks, and the way her gaze suddenly avoided meeting his.

The more time he spent in her company the more he realised what an enigma Joey was—one minute the sophisticate, the next blushing like a schoolgirl over a perfectly innocent remark.

A remark that no longer seemed quite so innocent...

'Joey?'

Her gaze settled in the vicinity of the middle of his chest. 'You're right. It is late—and we both have work in the morning—'

'Look at me, Joey,' Gideon cut in firmly.

Joey was looking at him. And liking—far too much—what she saw! She had always thought Gideon would be lean and muscled beneath those formal suits and silk shirts he always wore, and had been increasingly aware throughout the evening of just how attractive he looked in that fitted black cashmere sweater and tailored black trousers.

To her dismay, she could once again feel the revealing hardening of her nipples as they rubbed against the soft wool of her own sweater, and the less visually obvious aching arousal between her thighs. Joey didn't dare so much as look at Gideon's face now, knowing that if she saw awareness in his own expression she would be well and truly lost.

She flicked her tongue nervously across her lips. 'I'm sorry I wasn't of any help with—Gideon...!'

Her gasp was breathily panicked as she was suddenly pulled into his arms, her gaze alarmed as she finally looked up at him.

Oh, help...

His eyes were that pure molten gold as he looked down searchingly into her face. There was a telling, aroused flush along those high, aristocratic cheekbones, and his lips—those sensually sculptured, perfectly delicious lips—were slightly parted, as if he were about to kiss her!

Gideon would be lying to himself as well as to Joey if he were to claim that he hadn't known from the moment he'd arrived at her apartment that this was going to happen. The whole time the disks had been playing he had been watching her from beneath lowered lids, rather than the television screen. Watching. And waiting. The hardness of his arousal becoming a pulsing ache as the minutes slowly ticked by.

He wanted Joey McKinley.

Damn it, he didn't just want her. His desire for her had reached a point where he *had* to have her!

There were too many complications, he reminded himself cautiously. His twin brother was married to her twin sister. Their two families were connected by that marriage. An affair between the two of them would be a problem—especially when it ended. Whether the affair ended amicably or badly, Gideon knew the memory of it would linger for both of them, making it uncomfortable for them to attend family occasions together.

Unfortunately none of those things mattered a damn now, when Gideon burned to take her to bed and make love to her in every way possible.

And Joey's response earlier had already shown him that she returned that desire, at least...

Maybe desire was the real basis for their dislike of each other? Maybe if they made love together it would ease that tension rather than heighten it—?

Who the hell was he trying to kid? At this moment he couldn't care less what happened after he and Joey had made love, as long as they *did*!

He held her gaze with his. 'In a few moments I'm going to strip every article of clothing from your body, and then have you do the same to me, before carrying you into your bedroom and making love to you. If that isn't what you want too, then you had better say so now.'

Joey looked up at Gideon searchingly, knowing by the complete lack of embellishment to his words that it was a statement of intent rather than a declaration of feelings. Oh, there was desire, of course—Joey now knew exactly what emotion the glittering gold of Gideon's eyes signified! But that was all this was. A desire to make love to her.

Was it the same desire she felt for Gideon?

Maybe. No—not maybe. She *did* desire him. More than she had ever wanted or desired any other man, if her response earlier was any indication. But Joey had always believed that when she made love for the first time it would be with a man who loved her and whom she loved in return. She wanted that even more now that she had seen the happiness her twin had found in loving Jordan and having that love reciprocated. Their commitment to each other was absolute.

She and Gideon didn't have any of that.

What they did have—would always have—was a family connection from Stephanie and Jordan's marriage. As well as a commitment from Joey to work at St Claire's for the next three and a half weeks, of course!

She pulled back slightly to look up at Gideon with guarded eyes. 'Does this blunt, no-nonsense approach usually work for you?'

Gideon scowled darkly. 'I have always believed in honesty in my personal relationships, yes.'

Joey shrugged. 'There's honesty,' she said, 'and then there's cold, hard logic. I'm sure in other circumstances the first is commendable,' she said dryly. 'But I have to tell you that cold, hard logic coming from a potential lover isn't in the least appealing.'

Gideon's jaw tensed. 'Damn it, Joey, I can see how much you want me!' He looked down to where her nipples stood out revealingly against her sweater.

Her chin rose and her gaze steadily met the burning gold of those stunning eyes. 'Wanting something doesn't always mean it's wise to take it.' She twisted out of his arms to step away from him. 'Believe me, Gideon, when you wake up alone in your own bed tomorrow morning, you'll thank me for saying no tonight.'

Somehow he doubted that very much! He also doubted this constant state of arousal whenever he was in her company—damn it, even when he was *out* of it too—was going to go away any time soon.

But perhaps, for all the reasons he had already told himself, Joey was right to shy away from any deeper involvement between the two of them... *Damn it*!

He thrust his hands into his trouser pockets. 'You're right, of course,' he admitted distantly.

'I am?' She tried teasing. 'That must be a first for me where you're concerned. I should make a note of it in my diary—'

'Don't push it, hmm, Joey?' Gideon said.

Joey was so relieved to have the tension eased between them, and in a way that hadn't caused too much embarrassment to either of them, that she could only grin up at him. 'Do you want that coffee, or do you have to go now?'

Derision sparked in his eyes. 'What do you think?'

'I think I'll see you in morning.'

'Actually, you won't.' He shook his head. 'That was another reason I decided to come here tonight. I had forgotten I'm driving to Oxford in the morning, for a ten o'clock appointment with the owner of a family-run hotel there that Lucan is considering taking into our existing chain.'

'Oh.' Joey nodded. It was the most knowledge concerning St Claire's that Gideon had confided to her in the past three days; the man gave a whole new meaning to playing things close to his chest. 'Do you need me to come with you?'

'Not at this stage, no.'

'I'll see you later in the day, then?'

Again Gideon shook his head. 'I don't work at St Claire's on Thursday afternoons.'

'You don't?'

'It's a long-standing agreement with Lucan.'

Joey eyed him speculatively. 'What *do* you do on Thursday afternoons? Or shouldn't I ask?'

Gideon's gaze was just as direct as her question. 'You shouldn't ask.'

Joey had meant the remark teasingly, but obviously Gideon had taken it literally. Now she was curious—what did he do on Thursday afternoons that was so secret?

Joey was so intrigued by the puzzle that, long after he'd left, she tried to guess what possible incentive could take him away from St Claire's each week.

With any other man Joey would have said it was a woman, perhaps a married one, he could only see on a Thursday afternoon when her husband was away or at work. But as the man was Gideon, she somehow didn't think that was the right explanation.

For one thing he was something of a workaholic, with his own life and emotions taking second place to that dedication. Taking an afternoon off from that work in order to spend time in bed with his married mistress would, Joey felt sure, be complete anathema to a man like him. Or perhaps she just hoped that it would?

More to the point, Gideon's own parents' marriage had broken down because of his father's relationship with another woman, and it had succeeded in emotionally scarring all three of the St Claire brothers. Even if Gideon found himself attracted to a married woman, Joey somehow couldn't see him ever giving in to that attraction.

She was so intrigued by the mystery of what he did on a Thursday afternoon, that it wasn't until after she had gone to bed and fallen asleep that the possible answer to that other, more pressing puzzle of who might have vandalised their two cars, literally came to her in a dream...

CHAPTER SEVEN

JOEY was literally jumping up and down in frustrated excitement by the time Gideon arrived at St Claire's at eight-thirty on Friday morning. Looking his usual cool and aloof self, in a charcoal-grey suit, white shirt and pale grey silk tie, rather than like a man who had might possibly have spent yesterday afternoon in bed with his married mistress—whatever that might look like!

Was that a sense of relief Joey was feeling?

If it was, then it was entirely inappropriate. She'd had her chance on Wednesday evening if she'd wanted to go to bed with Gideon, making any feelings of jealousy on her part over where he went on Thursday afternoons completely ridiculous.

Which wasn't to say that she hadn't casually tried to find out if May knew what Gideon did every Thursday afternoon...

Either the woman didn't know the answer to that question, or she simply wasn't willing to share the information; whichever it was, despite casually mentioning the subject to both secretaries, by Friday morning Joey was still none the wiser as to where he went!

Gideon came to a halt in the doorway as soon as he saw Joey, standing beside the desk in Lucan's office. 'I thought your office was next door?'

She gave an impatient squeak which made him raise an amused blond brow in query. 'I needed to talk to you as soon as you got in.'

Gideon strolled farther into the room to place his briefcase beside the desk before turning to look at her. 'What could possibly be so urgent that you felt the need to ambush me as soon as I walked in the door?' He leant back on the front of the desk; yesterday had been a long and tiring day—not least because of the need to try and banish from his mind the unsatisfactory ending to the evening before, regarding the unlooked-for and unwanted desire he felt for Joey.

A desire that had, unfortunately, leapt into

being the moment Gideon set eyes on her again just now...

Joey was looking especially attractive today, in a red business suit and snowy white silk blouse. Her legs were long and silky beneath a pert short skirt, and she wore matching red high-heeled shoes—the latter still surprisingly on her feet, at the moment.

Why *this* woman? Gideon asked himself for what had to be the hundredth time. Why was it that just looking at Joey McKinley instantly took his thoughts to long, naked bodies stretched out invitingly on red satin sheets? Whatever it was, Gideon had every intention of mastering it rather than allowing it to master him.

Joey's jade-green eyes glowed with repressed excitement. 'I think I know who vandalised our cars. Well...I don't know his name or anything. But I do know what he looks like. I think...' She frowned in brief uncertainty before once again brightening. 'Well, I asked around the building, and no one seemed to know who I was talking about, and then I managed to walk casually onto every floor myself to see if I could see him working in any of the offices, but I couldn't, so—'

'Joey, could you take a couple of deep breaths and start again? From the beginning, if possible?' Gideon said, finally managing to interrupt her flow of words. 'You really aren't making a lot of sense at the moment,' he added, as she looked at him with frowning irritation.

She *had* been babbling, Joey acknowledged, taking a deep breath and willing herself to just calm down; she never babbled—and certainly not in front of Gideon St Claire! Besides, she only thought she *might* have solved the riddle of who had deliberately punctured the tyres on both her own car and Gideon's.

Speaking of which... 'Did you get your car back yet?'

Gideon nodded. 'Yesterday evening.'

'That's good. And the security disks we looked at the other evening? Do you have those with you now?'

Joey had gone down to Security herself and asked to look at the disks again, but the supervisor there had been unwilling to let her do that without Gideon's permission. It was understandable, but it would have made her enquiries so much easier if she could have had a printed photograph to show around and see if anyone recognised the person caught on camera.

Gideon's expression darkened. 'They're still in my briefcase. Why?'

'Because I think I might know—' Joey broke off, determined not to start babbling again.

The beginning, Joey, she instructed herself firmly. Start at the beginning. Calmly. Logically. That last one should be something that Gideon recognised, at least!

'As you know, I went to the coffee shop on Monday morning—'

'To see the buff and golden-haired young god— yes, I remember.' Gideon eyed her mockingly.

Joey shot him a glare. 'Will you just forget about him?'

'*I'm* not the one who's obsessed with him!'

Neither was she, really; at the time it had just been another way of teasing Gideon for being so uptight. A teasing that seemed to have backfired on her, if he was going to keep bringing it into every conversation...

'Forget him, okay?' she instructed irritably. 'It's the other man I met on Monday that I want to talk about—'

'Good God, Joey, how many men are involved in this balancing act you call your social life?' Gideon stood up abruptly and went to sit behind the desk, his eyes narrowed as he looked up at her. 'You already regularly date Jason Pickard, and lust after the golden-haired youth with stamina who serves you with your hot chocolate.' He gave a disgusted shake of his head. 'Apparently there's now another man to add to that list.'

And all of them could just as easily be dismissed—because she wasn't romantically involved with any of them.

'I believe you missed yourself off the list,' she retorted a little snidely.

'Perhaps that's as well,' he bit out.

'No doubt,' Joey said. 'The thing is, I remember seeing this particular man on one of those security disks we looked at on Wednesday evening. Around lunchtime, entering the car park on foot,' she added as Gideon opened his briefcase to look for the discs. 'Now, it could all be perfectly innocent,' she said cautiously, 'but when he spoke to me I remember thinking that he seemed slightly familiar—which again might just mean I've seen him here somewhere.'

'This man actually spoke to you?' Gideon closed his briefcase with a decisive snap, eyes dark with disapproval.

She grimaced. 'I spoke to him first, when I apologised for holding him up in the queue.'

'No doubt you were distracted at the time, drooling over the—'

'Gideon, I swear, if you mention the buff twenty-year-old *one more time*, I'm afraid I will really have to become violent!' Joey was very aware that it had been *Gideon*, the seriously buff thirty-four-year-old, who had been responsible for her distraction on Monday morning, rather than someone barely out of adolescence!

His expression was derisive. 'I'll forget about him if you will.'

'Consider him forgotten!' she said through gritted teeth. 'So, I apologised to this man for delaying him and then left, but I was still standing on the pavement outside when he came out, which was when he talked to me—'

'Understandably,' Gideon interjected. 'You had given him an opening earlier, and you're a very beautiful woman.' He shrugged when Joey gave him a questioning look. 'Well, you are,' he mocked lightly as her glance became quelling.

Joey eyed him uncertainly. 'You didn't always seem to think so.'

His jaw tensed. 'I've never denied that you're a beautiful woman, Joey.'

'Just not one any sane man should ever be attracted to, hmm?'

He scowled. 'If that's the case, then it would seem I've joined the ranks of the insane.'

And Joey, having changed her opinion of Gideon being a cold and stuck-up aristocrat, also had to be out of her mind!

'Maybe we should just forget about that too?' she suggested.

He arched blond brows. 'For the moment? Or indefinitely?'

'Gideon, are you being deliberately awkward, or am I just imagining it?' She glared at him in frustration.

No, he conceded ruefully, she wasn't imagining anything. He had just been thrown slightly by the strength of his protective reaction on hearing that some strange man had obviously tried to pick her up.

It was because she was Stephanie's sister, he told himself. That connection made Joey 'family', and as such under the protection of the St Claires. It had absolutely nothing to do with his own illogical attraction to her. Nothing at all...

'Sorry,' he said, aware she was still waiting for a reply. 'So this man spoke to you?'

'It seemed perfectly natural at the time,' she said, obviously accepting his apology. 'How the changeable weather was causing colds, et cetera. But he also asked me if I worked locally—'

'You didn't tell him, did you?' he barked.

'Gideon, will you give me credit for having *some* intelligence?' She gave him a fierce frown.

'Sorry,' he muttered again.

'Of course I didn't tell him where I worked,' Joey continued calmly. 'But I do remember at the time making a conscious effort not to do so. Almost as if I somehow knew that I shouldn't.' She frowned. 'I excused myself as quickly as possible, but I remember feeling as if he was watching me as I walked away— What now?' she asked, when she saw Gideon's knowing expression.

He shook his head. 'I'm just surprised you would find that behaviour strange. Any red-blooded man would feel the same temptation to watch you as you walk away in those sexy high-heeled shoes.' He eyed her as he leant back in the chair. 'And do you have any idea how much like my mother you sound when you talk in that scolding tone of voice?'

'That's probably because—no doubt, *exactly* like your mother—I'm tempted to smack you every time you do or say something aggravating!'

Gideon smiled. 'My mother didn't believe in smacking any of her sons.'

'That probably explains why you, at least, have grown into such an annoying adult.'

Gideon found himself chuckling softly as he answered her. 'What's *your* excuse?'

'Oh, my ability to aggravate and annoy just comes naturally,' she assured him dryly.

Gideon laughed outright this time. Something he seemed to do quite a lot of around Joey, he found himself thinking.

'Well, at least I know when I'm being annoying,' Joey defended.

'Unlike some people?'

'Exactly!'

'In your case, you do it regardless,' Gideon accused.

She grinned. 'Of course.'

'Especially where I'm concerned.'

'Oh, especially then.' She nodded unabashedly. 'It's just too irresistible when you're so easy to tease.'

He looked rueful. 'Most people would know better than to even attempt it.'

Joey shrugged. 'I've already told you—I'm not most people.'

No, she certainly wasn't. Joey McKinley was unlike anyone else—certainly any other woman—Gideon had ever met.

'Perhaps we should just look at the disk for lunchtime?' He took out his laptop to place it on top of the desk and turn it on.

Joey was thrown slightly by the sudden change of conversation. Although why she should be, she had no idea; Gideon had proved, time and time again, how adept he was at avoiding subjects he didn't wish to talk about.

Talking of which...

'Did you do anything nice on your afternoon off yesterday?' She deliberately kept her tone lightly enquiring, having no intention of letting him see how consumed with curiosity she really was regarding his whereabouts.

He glanced at her over the top of his laptop, his expression inscrutable as he answered. 'I did what I usually do on a Thursday afternoon.'

'Which is?' Joey definitely had a problem imagining a workaholic like Gideon actually taking an afternoon off work to visit a mistress— or maybe that was just wishful thinking on her part? An aversion to even imagining him spending the afternoon in bed with another woman?

Which was pretty stupid when she could have gone to bed with him herself on Wednesday night. Something that still sent quivers of awareness down the length of her spine…

'Why the interest?' Gideon asked directly.

Joey shrugged. 'It just seems…out of character for you, and that intrigues me.'

'Really?' Gideon drawled.

'Okay—fine.' Joey held up her hands in surrender. 'If you want me to continue to think you spend Thursday afternoons in bed with your married mistress—'

'If I want you to carry on thinking *what*?' Gideon spluttered incredulously.

Joey's cheeks warmed as she saw the disbelief in his expression. Proof, if she had needed it, that she was way off the mark with the mistress remark. 'It was just a thought...'

'I'm not sure whether I should feel insulted or flattered,' Gideon grated. 'Maybe, as a precaution against allowing your imagination to run even wilder than it already has, I should tell you I deal with...other legal matters on Thursday afternoons.'

Joey blinked. That certainly hadn't been in her list of possibilities when she'd been considering Gideon's Thursday afternoon activities!

'I didn't know you still had a private practice.'

Gideon looked as if he wished he had never started this conversation, his jaw tense. 'I don't.'

'Then I don't understand.'

He sighed heavily. 'Do you really *need* to understand?'

'I think so, yes.'

Gideon continued to look at her for several long seconds before giving in. 'Purely in the interest of keeping you quiet, I'll tell you. I've helped to run a free legal advice clinic here in the city for the last couple of years.' He shrugged casually. 'See—no big secret. And no mistress—married or otherwise!'

'Oh.' It was so *not* what Joey had been expecting that she couldn't think of anything else to say.

'Yes—*oh*,' Gideon echoed dryly. 'Now, could we stop wasting time and just look at the appropriate disk?'

In other words, end of subject. Joey understood that as she moved around the desk to stand beside him. But it didn't stop her thinking. From realising that she had once again misjudged him…

She was so close to him now that she could take in tantalising breaths of clean male overlaid with an elusive tangy aftershave. Close enough to become uncomfortably aware of the heat of his body. Of how one of them only had to move slightly in order for them to be touching…

Stop it, Joey, she instructed herself firmly, even

as she moved as far away from Gideon as it was possible for her to be and still be able to see the screen of his laptop. What was wrong with her? She and Gideon had absolutely nothing in common. Well...that wasn't quite true, was it? They were both twins. Both valued their family. Liked their independence. Were both focused on their work—to the extent that Gideon actually helped run a free legal clinic, which she deeply admired.

Just those four things alone were more than some couples who had been married for years had in common!

'Joey, are you paying attention?'

She gave a guilty start as she realised that Gideon had been playing the disk while her thoughts wandered.

'Of course I'm paying attention,' Joey said mendaciously. 'I'll tell you when we get to the relevant part—*there*!' she shouted excitedly as the image came onto the screen. Her hands moved instinctively to grip Gideon's shoulder. And as quickly she removed them again once she realised what she had done. 'Sorry,' she muttered awkwardly.

Gideon glanced up at her curiously, surprised to see the slight flush to her cheeks, and the way her downcast gaze avoided meeting his own. Almost as if…

'Joey, if you would like to rethink your decision of Wednesday evening—and despite the wildness of your earlier imaginings—I'm still open to the idea.' He swivelled his chair so that she now stood between his parted legs.

Joey raised startled eyes, a frown creasing her creamy brow, her breasts rapidly rising and falling beneath the white silk of her blouse. 'I thought we had agreed it isn't a good idea for us to become involved?'

They had. And it wasn't. Not two days ago. Not now.

Except Gideon had only needed to take one look at Joey again this morning for all the pent-up desire of the past few days to once again attack every one of his senses. Damn it, he would only be trying to deceive himself if he didn't admit he had spent every one of the past thirty-six hours aching to make love to her.

He held her gaze with his as his arms moved about her waist, to slowly pull her towards him until the warm dip of her thighs rested against his erection, Joey's breasts beneath the silk blouse warm and soft against the hardness of his shirted chest, her lips only inches away from his.

'I want to take you right here and right now,' he rasped harshly.

Joey moistened suddenly dry lips, her hands once again resting on his shoulders, this time in a feeble effort to try and keep her distance. 'You do?' she whispered.

'Oh, yes,' Gideon admitted throatily.

She still wanted him too—needed him to assuage this constant burning ache inside her. Yet... 'I seem to remember we were interrupted the last time we tried this here,' she protested.

'I'll lock the doors,' he murmured.

'There's still the window...'

'The window?' Gideon's gaze moved past her incredulously, to the huge picture window.

Joey nodded. They might be ten floors up, but the building across the street was nine floors high, and had a roof garden that Joey had seen several of the employees there step out onto over the past few days, whenever they wanted a cigarette. As if to prove her point, right at that moment a couple of men appeared on the roof opposite.

Gideon frowned his irritation. 'Then we'll go into the adjoining bathroom and lock the damned door!'

Joey's cheeks burned. 'Wouldn't that look…a little strange, if May should come in here?'

Gideon's eyes glittered a deep burnished gold as he stood up. 'Who the hell cares how it looks?' He retained a tight grip on Joey's wrist as he led the way into a huge private bathroom she hadn't even realised was through this door from Lucan's office.

And it truly *was* a bathroom, Joey noted slightly dazedly as she looked around them. With a huge smoky-glass-sided shower in one corner, a marble bench seat beside it, and two sinks against the mirrored wall opposite. The walls and floor were also covered in mellow terracotta and cream marble, and the fittings were all in gold, with huge brown bath towels draped over a warm towel rail.

Gideon shut and locked the door behind them, before turning to press Joey back against the marble wall, his whole body tense as he lowered his head and his mouth captured hers for the first time.

Not roughly or demandingly, as Joey would have expected, but with a raw, absorbing sensuality that she had no will or desire to resist.

His mouth sipped from hers time and time again, his tongue a soft caress between her lips, before venturing deeper, claiming the heat of her mouth, and then retreating, only to claim her again. And again. Igniting a hunger inside her...a need for more.

Joey was too lost in those arousing kisses to protest as Gideon moved her slightly away from the wall to push her jacket down her arms, before discarding it completely. Her blouse quickly followed and Gideon broke the kiss long enough to gaze his fill of her breasts, cupped in a cream lacy bra, the nipples dusky-pink rosettes beneath that lace. He ran the soft pad of his thumb across their engorged tips.

'I want you naked, Joey,' he breathed huskily, and turned her so that she stood with her back towards him, facing the mirrored wall, his hands lightly cupping her breasts as he looked over her shoulder at their reflection.

Joey stared at that reflection too, her arousal deepening as she felt the warmth of Gideon's breath on her shoulder, the press of his arousal against the curve of her bottom where he stood so goldenly handsome behind her, his hands dark against her bra and much paler skin.

Gideon continued to hold her gaze with his as he lowered his head to move his mouth lightly against her throat, sipping, tasting. Joey's back arched invitingly as his hands tightened about her breasts, pushing them up so that they swelled temptingly over the cream lace.

'Unfasten your bra for me, Joey,' he encouraged huskily.

Joey continued to stare at their reflection in the mirror as she slowly reached behind her to unfasten the hooks of her bra, too mesmerised to be shocked at her behaviour, barely able to breathe as the hooks came loose. Only Gideon's cupping hands and the thin satin straps on her shoulders were keeping her bra in place now.

He didn't touch her in any other way as he kissed first one shoulder and then the other, nudging those thin straps down her arms and allowing the bra to fall away and bare her breasts completely.

His breath caught in his throat as he stared at Joey's reflection. Her breasts were full and tipped with temptingly beautiful dusky rose nipples, which became even harder, more swollen, as Gideon continued to look at them in the mirror.

'You're beautiful,' he breathed, stepping out from behind her to move her, so that she now sat on the marble bench seat, and pushing her skirt up her thighs so that he could kneel between her legs. He was able to feel the heat of her arousal as he cupped her breasts before bending to find first one dusky rose nipple and then the other with his mouth.

She tasted wonderful, her nipples swelling as Gideon drew on them hungrily, stroking with his tongue at the same time, all the while feeling Joey's trembling response as he allowed his teeth to gently scrape across those sensitive tips.

Joey was too lost in the vortex of pleasure to question why it was she was responding so totally to Gideon, of all men.

'Aren't you...a little overdressed still...?' she

prompted restlessly, desperate now to touch him in the same way he was touching her.

'A little.' He gave a rueful smile as he straightened, slipping out of his jacket and pulling off his tie before dropping them down on the floor with Joey's discarded clothes.

'Let me.' Joey gently pushed his hands away as he would have unbuttoned his shirt himself, and her gaze easily held his as she slowly unfastened each of those buttons. She only lowered it to look at him as she took off his shirt completely, to bare his tanned chest.

His shoulders were so wide, his muscled chest so clearly defined, with a light dusting of golden hair that dipped lower, to taper down beneath his trousers. Joey touched him lingeringly, running her fingers lightly over that tanned flesh. Gideon's nipples were hard little buds beneath her fingertips where they nestled amongst those golden curls.

Would kissing one give Gideon the same pleasure he had just given her? she wondered. She satisfied that curiosity, knowing by his sharply indrawn breath as he cupped the back of her head and held her against him that the answer to that question was a definite yes.

Emboldened, she turned to give the second hard bud the same treatment. His skin felt hot to the touch, and Joey was able to feel the rapid beating of Gideon's heart beneath her fingertips. Her hands moved lower, feeling the leap of his hard shaft as her fingers swept against him tentatively.

'God, yes, Joey…' Gideon groaned achingly, his hips pushing against her hands. Her caresses instantly became bolder at his encouragement, and she started to stroke the pulsing length of his erection harder and faster.

Gideon unbuttoned and unzipped his trousers himself, pushing them and his boxers down to his hips and instantly feeling relief as his arousal sprang free. He growled softly in his throat as he felt her hands taking possession of his bared flesh, instinctively thrusting into those caressing hands, knowing he was on the brink of release, and needing–oh, God—needing it so badly.

'Change places with me, Gideon,' Joey encouraged urgently, and she released him long enough for him to take her place on the marble seat. Now she knelt in front of him, stroking her tongue lightly across his sensitive tip, licking and tasting as her hand continued to stroke him firmly.

Gideon's vision became slightly blurred as he looked down and saw Joey taking him into her mouth, her slender fingers still curled about him, her tongue continuing that rasping, rhythmic swirl.

'I'm going to come if you don't stop!'

In complete contradiction of that warning Gideon moved one of his hands to the back of Joey's head, and his fingers became entangled in the glossy red of her hair, holding her to him as he instinctively began to thrust deeper. At the same time his other hand cupped and caressed one of her uptilting breasts, teasing, squeezing, before rolling the engorged nipple between finger and thumb.

Joey moaned in pleasure even as she felt the responsive warmth flood between her thighs.

She had never been this intimate with any man before. Never *wanted* to be this intimate with any man before Gideon. Had never felt this heady exhilaration at the giving and receiving of pleasure. Her caresses were purely instinctive...

'Yes, Joey…' Gideon's eyes glowed like molten gold between narrowed lids. 'Oh, God,' he groaned.

'Gideon?' A knock sounded on the bathroom door. 'Are you unwell, Gideon?' Concern could be clearly heard in May Randall's voice as she obviously stood on the other side of the locked bathroom door.

Joey froze, totally stricken, shocked at her complete lack of inhibition!

CHAPTER EIGHT

'OKAY, so you were proved right. Attempting to make love in a bathroom *wasn't* the most sensible thing I've ever thought of doing!'

Gideon paced Joey's office impatiently fifteen minutes later as she sat looking at him guardedly from behind her desk. Both of them were now fully dressed, and the pallor of her cheeks told him exactly how upset she still was.

Was is embarrassment at the depth of the intimacy they had shared earlier? Or disappointment because that intimacy had been interrupted? Gideon wasn't sure...

He did know that they had both reacted like guilty teenagers when May Randall knocked on the bathroom door. Joey's face had been stricken as she'd stood up to turn her back on him, quickly dressing in her cream lace bra and silk blouse. Gideon hadn't been much better as he'd forced his still aching erection back inside his boxers and zipped up his trousers. Tersely, he had assured May that he was fine, and would join her in her office in a few minutes, before pulling his shirt on and fastening the buttons with hands that had shaken slightly.

No, it certainly hadn't been Gideon's finest hour...

As he had just told Joey it hadn't been his most sensible one, either. Sadly, his usual cool sensibility had gone out of the window the moment she had come to work in the adjoining office!

'Will you please say something, Joey?' he pleaded now, at her continued uncomfortable silence.

Maybe she would break her silence if she could think of something to say. If she wasn't still so totally shocked by her own behaviour...

Ideally she needed to say something dismissive and sophisticated. But, as she didn't feel in the least dismissive *or* sophisticated at the moment, she had no idea what she could say without sounding ridiculously gauche and inexperienced.

Just looking at Gideon now, remembering the depth of the intimacy between them earlier, was enough to make her want to crawl away somewhere and hide. At least until she stopped feeling as if she might die from embarrassment every time she so much as looked at him. Which would be never...

Maybe the best thing was to just avoid the subject altogether. 'Have you had chance yet to look at that security disk?'

Gideon stopped his pacing to stare across the desk at her incredulously. 'Is that the best you can do?'

'I can see no benefit to either of us in talking about what just happened.' Especially as she was still in shock because of it!

Neither did he. Until, that was, Joey expressed her own reluctance to talk about it...

Just being near this woman made him behave recklessly, impulsively, illogically. Something he never, ever did—in any situation. Hearing her dismiss that behaviour as if it were of absolutely no consequence was enough to make him want to shake her!

He glowered down at her from the other side of the desk. 'How about we discuss a time when we can finish what we started?'

Green eyes met his briefly before Joey looked

quickly away again. 'That would be extremely stupid of us.'

'No more stupid than me walking about with a constant erection and you on the brink of orgasm!' he retorted.

Two bright wings of colour appeared in the pallor of her cheeks. 'You're being deliberately crude—'

'I'm being honest,' Gideon corrected.

'Then perhaps you ought to consider being less honest and a little more circumspect!' She glared up at him.

Gideon gave a humourless laugh. 'Until you came along, *circumspect* used to be my middle name. It seems to have abandoned me.'

'Then I suggest you find it again!'

She briskly shifted some papers on top of her desk, drawing Gideon's attention to the golden dragon sitting majestically at the front. Those glittering yellow eyes seemed to glower at him malevolently.

'Your good luck charm doesn't appear to be working at the moment,' he murmured ruefully.

'My good luck charm is working just fine.' Joey

reached out to touch the dragon defensively. 'It's the two of *us* who are behaving irrationally.'

Gideon looked slightly self-conscious. 'I have no more idea than you do what's going on between us.' He scowled his frustration. 'But something obviously is,' he added less forcefully as he gentled his expression. 'And we obviously can't keep doing this.'

Her fingers curled about the golden dragon. 'Doing what?'

'Going a little further each time we make love and then stopping.' He frowned darkly. 'Besides being frustrating as hell, it's totally disruptive!'

Joey smiled tightly. 'How typical that you should look at this from the point of view of how it affects your work—'

'Totally disruptive for both of us in regard to just living our lives,' he corrected her. 'Damn it, Joey, you're like a constant itch I can't scratch.'

'I believe that's the first time a man has compared me to having the irritation of a rash! How complimentary!' she said sarcastically.

'I don't recall using the word irritating.'

She shrugged. 'Nevertheless, it was there in your tone of voice.'

Gideon growled his impatience. 'You don't know me well enough yet to say *what's* in my tone of voice.'

'And I have no wish to know you well enough, either,' Joey stated firmly. 'Gideon, I can't stress strongly enough how much of a mistake I consider our earlier behaviour to be.' She met his gaze unflinchingly. 'Especially when you consider how much we dislike and disapprove of each other.'

Gideon became very still, his expression guarded, as he considered whether that statement was still true. In regard to himself, at least. He certainly hadn't liked or approved of Joey before she'd come to work with him. Right now he wasn't sure what he felt towards her...

'You're right, of course,' Gideon said calmly.

Joey looked up at him searchingly, unsure about his sudden capitulation. Gideon's expression was back to being cold and aloof, and revealed none of his real emotions.

Perhaps that was as well, considering how badly shaken she still was at the way they hadn't been able to keep their hands off each other the moment they saw each other again.

'And the answer to your earlier question is no—I haven't had a chance to look at the security disk yet,' he admitted. 'I thought—obviously mistakenly!—that it was more important for me come in here and offer you reassurance over what just happened rather than look at it.'

The inexperienced Joey would have welcomed his reassurance fifteen minutes ago—after May had first interrupted them. Now she just wanted to forget the whole embarrassing incident.

She gave a haughty inclination of her head. 'Obviously you *were* mistaken.'

Gideon dragged in a harsh breath and resisted the impulse he had to reach across the desk, grab hold of Joey's shoulders, and shake her until her teeth rattled—a move guaranteed, as it involved touching her, into tempting him into pulling her back into his arms. Which would take them God only knew where!

His jaw clenched as he ground his teeth together. 'Let's go and look at the damned thing now, if that's what you want.'

He turned on his heel and strode forcefully

into the adjoining office without waiting to see if Joey followed him. At that moment he didn't particularly care whether she did or not.

Gideon had known from the first that having her working here was going to cause unwanted complications—he just hadn't realised what direction those complications would take.

He always chose his bed partners with care— invariably because those women were able to regard physical relationships with the same detachment Gideon did. Yet just the smell of Joey's perfume, combining sexily aroused woman with a lightly floral scent, as she once again came to stand beside him as he brought up the image on his computer screen, was enough to cause a resurgence of his earlier arousal. So much for detachment, he thought frustratedly...

'I know him.' Gideon bent down for a closer look as the image she had frozen earlier, of a bearded man, reappeared on his computer screen. 'Where the hell do I know him from?'

'Maybe he works here after all?' Joey suggested helpfully.

'No, that isn't it.' Gideon continued to study the image. 'Maybe if we took away the beard?

Put a little weight on him? Possibly a shirt and tie—'

'And you'd have Richard Newman,' Joey said slowly.

Gideon glanced at her briefly, before turning his attention back to the man on the screen. 'We have Richard Newman,' he agreed.

The same Richard Newman who had been only too happy to let Joey's sister Stephanie be named as the other woman in his divorce a couple of months ago, in order to protect the woman he was really having an affair with—namely his boss's wife. Richard Newman who had subsequently lost his wife and custody of his children, his home and his mistress, and his job, when the truth finally came out.

A truth that Gideon and Joey, between them, had discovered and revealed…

Well…mainly Gideon, to be perfectly honest. But Joey had certainly been working towards proving her twin's innocence, too.

Which was perhaps why Newman had now chosen to target both of them with malicious sabotage?

Gideon turned to look at Joey, frowning slightly

as he saw that she had stepped away from the desk and now stood with her back towards him in front of the window, her arms wrapped almost protectively about her waist.

'Joey?'

She didn't answer, but her shoulders began to tremble.

Gideon pushed his chair back to stand up slowly. 'Joey, are you okay?'

'Am I *okay*?' she repeated sharply as she turned, those jade-green eyes glittering brightly. 'We almost made love in the damned bathroom, and now—'

'Let's just concentrate on Richard Newman,' Gideon muttered grimly.

She shook her head. 'They warned me about this when I took my law degree. The possibility that some dissatisfied client might one day turn nasty. But I never thought—I never imagined it would ever happen to me. Or realised how awful it would feel if it did.'

'Joey—'

'I *spoke* to him, Gideon!' Her voice broke emotionally, and her eyes were wide with distress now as the trembling intensified. 'I stood in front of him in the coffee shop, and when he came outside he deliberately engaged me in casual conversation. And all the time he— It can't have been a coincidence, Gideon. He must have been watching me. Must have followed me to the coffee shop! Deliberately stood behind me in the queue—oh, God…!' The trembling became full-blown shaking as the enormity of that supposedly casual meeting hit her.

Gideon had become so accustomed to Joey's perky self-confidence, the way she usually had an answer to everything and everyone, that for a few brief seconds he could only stand and stare at her rather than respond. Until those tears swimming in her jade-green eyes began to cascade over her lashes to fall hotly down her cheeks.

'Oh, Joey!' Gideon gave a pained groan as he stepped forward to enfold her in his arms and hold her tightly against him.

Joey clung to Gideon, knowing she had never felt so scared. Never felt as if her life, what was going on around her, was so totally out of her control.

How long had Richard Newman been following her? Just this past week, since she'd come to work at St Claire's? Or had it started before that? Had he been secretly watching her for weeks? Just waiting for the chance, the opportunity—

'Don't let your imagination run away with you, Joey,' Gideon advised evenly.

'Well, at least I can claim to *have* an imagination!' She moved back to glare up at him.

Gideon's mouth thinned as he recalled their conversation on Monday morning, when Joey had last accused him of lacking in imagination. 'Resorting to insulting me again isn't going to help this situation.'

'*Nothing* is going to help this situation!'

'I'll deal with it.'

'How?' Joey challenged. 'How will you deal with it, Gideon?' Her voice rose emotionally. 'I realise you're one of the invincible St Claires, but even so—'

'*Joey.*'

Joey stared at him for several long seconds before drawing in a deep, controlling breath. Gideon had only spoken her name, in that cool and calm way of his, but nevertheless it was enough to halt her rising hysteria.

'I'm sorry.' She released a shaky sigh. 'Instead

of insulting you I should really be congratulating myself—the fact that Newman only punctured one of my tyres to your two would seem to imply that he only hates me half as much as he hates you,' she explained ruefully when Gideon raised questioning brows.

'Glad to see you're getting your sense of humour back!' he murmured as his arms dropped back to his sides and he stepped away from her.

'That's me.' Joey nodded self-derisively. 'A laugh a minute!'

Gideon wasn't fooled for a moment. He had seen yet another side of Joey this morning. Beneath that tough exterior she chose to present to the world there was a woman every bit as soft and vulnerable as her twin. The woman who kept a golden dragon on her desk because her twin had given it to her. For good luck, she said. And the woman with a singing voice an angel would envy, which she chose not to share publicly. Knowing what he did of her now, Gideon was sure there was a perfectly good reason—an emotional reason—why that was.

Joey McKinley was the most complex and by

far the most fascinating woman Gideon had ever met…

That alone was enough to set off alarm bells inside him. The emotions she displayed were enough of a warning to keep his distance. Gideon had managed, for over twenty years to avoid all emotional entanglement, apart from with his close family, and the complex and deeply emotional Joey McKinley was in danger of breaching that carefully built-up detachment.

Gideon had learnt at a young age, after the break-up of his parents' marriage when he was ten years old, of the complexities and the danger of feeling emotion—particularly romantic love—for another person. His mother Molly had loved his father Alexander—only to learn, after thirteen years of marriage and the birth of three sons, that her husband had been in love with another woman for twenty years. The woman Alexander had eventually abandoned his wife and sons to be with.

Oh, Molly had seemed to finally come to terms with that when Lucan had announced he was marrying the granddaughter of the 'other woman' in that love triangle. But Gideon still clearly remembered the heartache his mother had suffered when she and Alexander had parted so acrimoniously. In all these years she had never even thought of falling in love again—let alone remarrying. It was a lesson in 'love' that all three of Molly's sons had taken to heart.

The fact that Jordan and Lucan had both succumbed in the past two months, and subsequently married the women they'd fallen in love with, in no way shook the decision Gideon had made over twenty years ago *never* to put his own heart into someone else's keeping just so that they could trample all over it.

He certainly wasn't about to break his own rule of remaining detached by allowing himself to feel any sort of emotion for the unpredictable Joey McKinley!

Apart, that was, from the desire that raged through him every time he so much as looked at her…

He moved to sit back behind his desk before Joey could become aware that he was once again aroused. 'I believe the best way to deal with this is for me to contact the police and tell them what we know. Once I have, they will probably want to talk to you, too.'

'I'm not going anywhere.' Joey had no idea what Gideon had been thinking about for the past few minutes, but whatever it was they hadn't been pleasant thoughts.

Not surprising, really, when the two of them had the problem of Richard Newman hanging over their heads like the Sword of Damocles. But, awful as that situation was, Joey felt a certain relief that it had at least diverted attention from their earlier passion.

That whole situation was getting completely out of hand—or *in* hand, as it had turned out; Joey wondered if she would ever be able to banish the memories of touching Gideon, and having him touch her as intimately, completely from her mind!

But she was going to have to do just that if she was to stand any chance of getting through the next three weeks of working with him so closely.

She straightened. 'I suggest we refrain from telling Stephanie or Jordan anything about this for the moment,' she said briskly. 'They can't do anything about it, and it would only worry Stephanie, and no doubt Jordan too, if they knew about it.'

Gideon raised derisive brows. 'I believe I have enough intelligence to have worked that out for myself.'

Joey had never doubted his intelligence— only his ability to empathise with other people. Although even *that* was questionable after the way he had kissed and caressed her to the brink of release earlier.

Her traitorous body still ached for that release. Her breasts chafed uncomfortably inside her bra, and her panties were damp and uncomfortable against the sensitive skin between her thighs…

She nodded abruptly. 'I'll leave you while you call the police.' She turned swiftly on her heel to walk to the doorway between their two offices.

'Joey…'

She came to an abrupt halt, determinedly schooling her features into mild curiosity before she turned back to face Gideon. 'Yes?'

'It's going to be all right, you know.' He gave her a reassuring smile. 'I'm not going to let Newman anywhere near you,' he added gently.

That gentleness was almost Joey's undoing, and as she once again felt that emotional lump rise to constrict her throat. She could deal with Gideon's coldness, his sarcasm, his detachment, even his unexpected passion, but his gentleness was something else entirely...

'We'll see,' she managed, before finally escaping into her own office.

Before she broke down a second time and decided to run back into the security of Gideon's protective arms and blubber all over him like a baby!

CHAPTER NINE

'I STILL think this is unnecessary,' Joey muttered grumpily as she got out of her car and locked it, before turning to face Gideon as the two of them stood in front of her apartment building.

'You heard the police advice.' He shrugged unapologetically as he joined her on the pavement, his own car parked directly behind Joey's. 'For the moment there's safety in numbers—which means I don't intend letting you drive to or from work again on your own, or indeed anywhere else, until they've managed to locate and question Newman.'

Yes, Joey had been present in Gideon's office when the two police officers, after learning of the events of the past few days, had offered that advice. She had even appreciated the practicality of that advice at the time; if she never went out alone then Newman wouldn't be able to accost her again, as he had at the coffee shop on Monday morning. But appreciating the practicality of the advice and actually living with it were two distinctly different things!

Especially now, after a day of having Gideon insist on accompanying her to the coffee shop this morning to collect her hot chocolate—with less than flattering remarks about the immaturity of the poor guy serving behind the counter!—and then again to the park nearby when she went out to eat her sandwich at lunchtime. Now, finally, he had followed her home in his own car to make sure she arrived safely.

All this 'togetherness' certainly wasn't going to make it any easier to forget what had happened between them that morning!

She pulled the strap of her bag firmly up onto her shoulder. 'I'm home now, Gideon,' she said pointedly, not feeling in the least reassured by the way he had locked and walked away from his own car just now.

His eyes narrowed. 'Are you intending to go out again?'

'What if I am?' Joey frowned. 'You aren't coming with me!' she exclaimed as she saw the determined expression on his face.

'That would depend on where you intend going, now, wouldn't it.'

Joey snorted her frustration. 'And if I'm going out on a date?'

Gideon's brows rose. 'Are you?'

'As it happens, no,' she said. 'I usually go to the gym on a Friday evening,' she added grudgingly.

He nodded. 'Then that's where we'll go.'

She sighed with impatience. 'Newman is hardly going to follow me there. You have to be a member to get in, for one thing—'

'Joey.'

Again Gideon only said her name—but it was done in such a way as to convey to her that he had no intention of doing anything other than what he chose to do. And at that moment he was choosing to accompany her to the gym.

'We haven't so much as set sight on the man for the past two days—'

'Which in no way guarantees that he won't decide to follow you again tonight,' Gideon reasoned.

'This is utterly ridiculous!'

Gideon had to hold back a smile at Joey's

obvious frustration with the situation. Not that he found the reason for this caution in the least amusing, but her response to it certainly was.

She had been obviously uncomfortable that morning, when he'd accompanied her to the coffee shop and given his opinion on the 'buff' young god serving behind the counter. She'd been equally ungracious when Gideon had chosen to eat his own lunch in the park with her—and then teased her mercilessly about illegally feeding most of her sandwich to the ducks. And he had to admit to enjoying her discomfort now, at the idea of his accompanying her to the gym.

Obviously his spending all this time in her company was far from ideal, after his earlier decision to keep his distance from her, but other than assigning her a bodyguard—something Joey would no doubt find even more unacceptable than their present arrangement—he couldn't think of any other solution to their present problem.

So, until the police had found and at least spoken to Richard Newman, the two of them appeared to be stuck with each other. And she would just have to accept it.

'How about I take you out to dinner afterwards?' he cajoled.

'Isn't that rather defeating the object of going to the gym?' Joey asked.

'Not if you have something healthy to eat, no.'

He was being deliberately irritating, Joey decided shrewdly. He was patently enjoying himself far too much—and at her expense! 'Look, Gideon—'

'No, *you* look, Joey,' he interrupted calmly. 'You and I both know that Stephanie would never forgive me if I didn't make sure nothing happens to you.'

Damn!

Damn, damn, *damn!*

Joey glared at him. He *would* have to invoke the 'Stephanie' word. A tactic that Gideon knew very well was guaranteed to silence all her protests. Much as Joey liked her independence, she would never do anything to disturb or disrupt her twin's newly married bliss to the gorgeous Jordan.

She couldn't help thinking that, for twins, the two men didn't look or behave anything alike.

Jordan was dark-haired and golden-eyed, and Gideon had blond hair and chocolate-brown eyes; Jordan was effortlessly charming, while Gideon's charm was much more subtle.

So much of Gideon, it seemed, was hidden beneath the surface. That deep love for his family. His concern two months ago for Stephanie. The way he was insisting on taking care of Joey right now...

Whatever the reason for Joey's attraction to him—and the more she came to know him the deeper the attraction became—she hoped that the police managed to find and talk to Richard Newman very soon. Because she wasn't sure how much of this togetherness with Gideon she could take without succumbing to the desire that raged through her every time she looked at him—when she wasn't annoyed with him, that was...

She gave him a reproving frown now. 'That's emotional blackmail.'

He appeared unconcerned by the accusation. 'So?'

Joey grumbled, 'It's absolutely shameful to use my love for Stephanie in this way.'

'Is it working?'

'Yes.'

'Mission accomplished.' Gideon gave an un-apologetic smile. 'I'll wait here while you go up and get your things.'

Wasn't this going to be a lot of fun? The whole point of Joey's thrice-weekly workout was to keep her fit, but it also involved her becoming hot and sweaty. Not something she particularly relished with Gideon looking on.

'You're wasting time, Joey,' he drawled mock-ingly, as if well aware of her discomforting thoughts.

Which no doubt he was! 'How about I sign you in as my guest, and you can join me instead of just keeping an eye on me?'

'Good idea,' he agreed. 'I usually go to my own gym every morning before work, so my stuff from this morning is still in the boot of my car.'

Well, that little ploy hadn't worked, had it? She should have guessed Gideon worked out in a gym on a regular basis; he obviously hadn't ac-quired that muscled chest and the taut power of the rest of his body, just by sitting behind a desk five days a week.

'Unless you think Jason Pickard might object to us spending the evening together?'

Joey's gaze sharpened suspiciously as she looked up at Gideon, but she was unable to read anything from his politely enquiring expression.

She wasn't deceived. 'I've already told you—you have completely the wrong idea about my friendship with Jason. It isn't like that.'

'You seem very determined that I should believe you.'

'Probably because I don't want you to go around thinking I allowed you to...to kiss me when I'm already involved with someone.'

Without breaking Jason's confidence, Joey had no way of convincing Gideon of that; Jason might have chosen to confide in his parents now about the true nature of his relationship with Trevor, but that didn't mean he wanted his very private life revealed to anyone else.

'I don't think that at all,' Gideon said. 'I believe I know you well enough by now to realise that double-dealing and two-timing just isn't your style.'

'Then why do you keep mentioning Jason?'

'I didn't realise you had the monopoly on teasing...'

Teasing? Gideon had been *teasing* her?

Joey stomped off, muttering, 'I've created a monster!'

Gideon's smile was rueful as he watched Joey from between narrowed lids as she walked to her apartment building, very aware of the sexy sway of her hips and silkily shapely legs before she opened the door and disappeared inside. In much the same way Richard Newman had been aware as he'd watched her walk away from the coffee shop on Monday morning...

Gideon's smile faded. Just thinking about the other man having been that close to her was enough to strengthen his resolve to protect her in spite of herself. He had been stating the truth when he'd claimed that Stephanie would never forgive him if anything happened to her twin sister, but it was equally true that Gideon would never forgive himself, either...

'Ready!'

Gideon focused on Joey with an effort as she appeared beside him in the promised five minutes, his eyes widening as he saw she had used that time to change into a fitted white T-shirt beneath a black sports cardigan, and baggy grey tracksuit bottoms that rested low down on her hips above white and purple trainers.

'You really are short, aren't you?' he commented. Once again, she reached only as high as his chin.

'Or you're just exceedingly tall.' She shot him an annoyed glance as she unlocked her car and threw her sports bag onto the back seat.

'Or I'm just exceedingly tall,' he allowed dryly as he dug his car keys out of his trouser pocket. 'You lead and I'll follow.'

'Now, there's an interesting suggestion,' she jeered.

'I think we've exhausted "interesting" for one day, don't you?' Gideon's smile was wry as he remembered the awkward way in which things had ended between them this morning.

'Probably.' She grimaced as she opened the driver's door of her car. 'I'll see you at the gym.'

Joey was very aware as she drove, as she had been earlier, of Gideon's car a short distance behind her own—probably to ensure that no one cut in between their two cars; she could clearly see Gideon in the driving mirror every time she glanced at it. In fact, she was so focused on Gideon driving behind her that she doubted she would have noticed Richard Newman if he had been sitting beside her!

Much as she might protest the necessity of having Gideon accompany her everywhere like this, she was grateful to him for bothering— even if his only reason for doing so was because Stephanie would never forgive him if he didn't.

She felt less grateful for that attentiveness an hour and a half later, when they met up in the bar for a reviving fruit drink at the end of their workout, and saw that he had barely broken a sweat despite the rigorous routine that she had witnessed surreptitiously as she'd moved around the apparatus in the gym—whereas Joey was dripping wet and very red in the face from her own exertions.

Looking at Gideon, dressed in a black vest top that showed the width of his shoulders and the defined muscles in his chest, and a pair of long black shorts that emphasised the muscled length of his legs, wasn't doing a lot to moderate her heart rate, either!

Several other women in the bar were eyeing him appreciatively too. Glances that Gideon, admittedly, seemed completely unaware of as he sipped his orange juice. Although she very much doubted that was because he was bowled off his feet by her own sweaty appearance!

'Have you heard from Lucan at all?' Joey abruptly filled the silence that—for her at least—was starting to stretch awkwardly between them; in contrast, Gideon seemed perfectly relaxed and at ease as he sipped his juice.

Gideon raised mocking brows. 'He's on his honeymoon, Joey. Of course I haven't.'

'Well...yes.' She felt warmth colour her cheeks—as if they needed to be any redder! 'I just thought...' She grimaced; she hadn't been thinking at all. Of *course* Lucan was on his honeymoon—and recalling the broodingly sensual way in which he had been looking at his bride at their wedding, they had probably spent all of the time so far in bed!

Gideon took pity on Joey's discomfort as he chuckled softly. 'You just thought, because Lucan has always been a workaholic, that he wouldn't be able to resist telephoning me to check on things, anyway?'

'All you St Claire men are the same when it comes to your work.'

He shrugged. 'I'm guessing the beautiful Lexie has given my big brother a different perspective on what his priorities are in life. Just as Stephanie has Jordan,' Gideon added with a frown, knowing he was still coming to terms with those particular changes in his two brothers.

For so long it had been just the three of them, united against the world during those long, interminable visits to their father—until they'd reached an age where they could choose not to go, and didn't. Then the years they had spent at university and the three of them had been there for each other when they'd entered their chosen careers. Then Jordan had fallen in love with and married Stephanie, and Lucan had met and fallen in love with Lexie. Giving Gideon's brothers a different focus in their lives in an incredibly short space of time.

It was utterly ridiculous of Gideon to feel as if

Jordan and Lucan had somehow left him behind. Especially when he had no more interest now in falling in love or getting married than he'd ever had—which was no interest whatsoever. He sincerely hoped that the desire he now felt for Joey was only a temporary aberration...

But desire her he did. Even now, obviously hot and glowing from her time in the gym, Joey somehow managed to look desirable, in a fitted white sports top that clearly defined her bared breasts beneath, and left a six-inch expanse of her flat stomach bare. She had removed the grey sweats to reveal black Spandex sports shorts that clung to the slenderness of her hips and thighs and the tautness of her bottom; he obviously couldn't see the latter at the moment, but he'd had plenty of opportunity to watch her earlier, as she'd moved around the gym. It was an opportunity he had taken full advantage of, admiring the slender curves of her body as she exercised—

Damn it—that was enough!

'Time we both showered, I think.' Gideon sat forward suddenly, and placed his empty glass on the table.

Joey couldn't speak for several seconds as she was instantly assailed with an image of the two of them together in the shower, completely naked, as she lathered soap over every delectable inch of Gideon's muscled body...

Which she was pretty sure wasn't what he had meant at all!

Joey gave herself a mental shake as she placed her own empty glass on the table beside his. 'Good idea. I'll meet you downstairs in Reception afterwards.'

She stood up to hurry away to the ladies' changing rooms—before Gideon had the chance to notice, and question, the sudden heat that had returned to her cheeks.

What was wrong with her? She couldn't seem to spend a single moment in his company any more without her thoughts turning to the bedroom—or, in their case, the bathroom!

Get a grip, Joey, she instructed herself firmly. Gideon was only spending his leisure time with her because he felt a family obligation to keep his sister-in-law's twin safe. It wasn't Joey personally he was concerned about. It was just that strong St Claire gentlemanly code of honour dictating that he ensured no harm came to her. Something she would do well to remember...

Joey felt refreshed and fortified by the time she rejoined Gideon in Reception fifteen minutes later. Her hair was still damp from the shower, and falling softly onto her brow and nape, but she felt far less exposed in a cream fitted sweater and figure-hugging low-riding jeans than she had in her sports gear.

Gideon, on the other hand, was once again dressed in the tailored business suit he had worn to work earlier. Although he *had* left off the tie and unbuttoned the top two buttons of his white silk shirt.

Joey felt a little self-conscious. 'I think I'm a little under-dressed to go out to dinner.'

'Or I'm over-dressed.' Gideon smiled.

Joey's stomach lurched, and her heart pounded loudly in her chest. So much for fortification— Gideon only had to smile at her and she was once again a quivering mass of desire!

'Maybe I should go home and change first?' he added at her continued silence.

She shrugged. 'I can always meet you some-where—'

'Not an option, I'm afraid.'

'But—'

'Come with me.'

Joey blinked. 'Come with you where?'

'To my apartment, of course.' Gideon looked down at her, noting how soft her red hair was without the gel she usually applied to achieve that wispy style. Her face was bare of make-up too, after her shower.

Although he wasn't quite sure about the hor-rified expression that had appeared on her face at his suggestion that she accompany him to his apartment to wait for him while he changed before they went out to dinner!

It probably *wasn't* a good idea, now that he thought about it. In fact he had no idea why he had even suggested it in the first place; he didn't take women to his apartment. *Any* woman. Not even one he had offered his protection. Most especially when Gideon had the distinct feeling that *he* was the one Joey might need protection from once they were alone together…

'Never mind,' he said. 'We're only going to

grab something quick to eat at a bistro, or somewhere equally as casual, before I make sure you
get home safely, so I don't suppose it really matters what I'm wearing.'

'No! No, I— It's fine if we go to your apartment first,' Joey said, slightly breathlessly, her
curiosity about Gideon's home overriding her
good sense in regard to whether or not it was
actually a good idea for her to go anywhere near
the privacy of his apartment with him.

She was curious to know if his home was as
lacking in complications as the rest of his life
appeared to be...

'I can guarantee you won't like the white decor,
or the chrome and black furnishings in my apartment,' Gideon said with a brief smile, guessing
her thoughts.

'You don't sound as if you like them very much
yourself.' Joey looked up at him thoughtfully
as they stepped outside. Gideon's face appeared
grim in the single spotlight illuminating the
Tarmacked area behind the gym where they had
parked their cars earlier.

'It was already decorated that way when I
bought the apartment.' He gave a dismissive

shrug. 'It serves its purpose in giving me somewhere to lay my head at night.'

'And is that—'

'It's functional, Joey, which is all I've ever needed or wanted it to be,' he said with finality, before striding across the Tarmac to his car.

Definite end of subject, Joey acknowledged ruefully as she followed more slowly, knowing a sense of disappointment that Gideon's home was as sterile of sentimentality as she had imagined it might be.

'Damn!' Gideon's angry outburst interrupted Joey's thoughts. 'Damn, damn and double damn!'

'What is it?' She hurried over to where he stood beside his car. 'What's happened—?' She broke off abruptly as she saw for herself exactly what had happened: a single, long and jagged gouge had been made all the way down the driver's side of his car. 'Oh, no!' she breathed.

'Oh, yes,' Gideon confirmed grimly as he turned his attention to Joey's car parked beside his own.

He came to a halt as he saw there was an identical gouge, deep and jagged, on the driver's side of her Mini.

Gideon was pretty sure they both knew who was responsible for the damage....

CHAPTER TEN

'DRINK up, Joey,' Gideon encouraged as he handed her one of the two glasses of brandy he had just poured. 'You'll feel better if you drink all of it,' he instructed firmly when she only took a tentative sip.

It was over an hour since they had left the gym and discovered the damage to the cars. An hour, during which the same two policemen they had spoken to earlier had driven out to the car park to assess and give their professional opinion of this second act of vandalism.

The use of the St Claire name earlier today had obviously had some effect on their efficiency.

The policemen had then offered their regrets that they obviously hadn't yet managed to locate Richard Newman, let alone talk to him; that apology seemed to confirm that they also believed the man to be responsible for the deep gouges in the paintwork of the two cars.

By the time the police left, Gideon had seen that Joey didn't look at all her usual perky, confident self: her face had been pale, her hands— all of her, in fact—trembling almost uncontrollably. Her distress had been confirmed by the fact that she had raised no objections to his suggestion that they leave her car where it was for the moment and he would drive them both back to his apartment.

Despite his earlier aversion to that idea, it had seemed the wisest choice in the circumstances. His apartment building had a doorman downstairs and security cameras installed, and Joey's obviously didn't. Besides which, Gideon had no idea whether she had any reviving brandy in her apartment, and there was no doubt they were both in need of something after the shock of finding their cars deliberately damaged.

The red of Joey's hair was the only real colour in the Spartan comfort of Gideon's sitting room. It comprised a glass and chrome coffee table sided by a black leather couch and two chairs, black and white prints in chrome frames hanging on the white-painted walls, a chrome and onyx standard lamp behind the couch, and a matching light overhead in the centre of the room.

His own and Joey's apartments were as different as the moon from the sun. Hers had all the warmth and comfort that made it a home, rather than just somewhere to store clothes and sleep at night...

Joey shook her head. 'I don't understand why Newman has waited until now. If it is him doing these things—and I'm inclined to think that it is—' she shuddered as she once again remembered actually talking to the man on Monday morning '—it's been over two months since we—well, mainly you—' she shot Gideon a rueful glance '—extracted Steph from any involvement in the Newmans' divorce.'

Gideon nodded grimly. 'I didn't understand the timing of this thing either, so I did some checking earlier today. The Newmans' divorce went to court last Friday. Rosalind Newman went for everything she could get—including custody of the two children, with only agreed access for Richard Newman. It would seem to be a case of "hell hath no fury" etc...'

'I'm inclined to think Rosalind Newman's

fury was justified where her ex-husband is con-cerned!' Joey exclaimed, the brandy having re-vived her somewhat.

Enough for her to recognise that he had brought her back to his apartment after all...

An apartment that, with its white decor and black and chrome furniture, was as impersonal as Gideon had warned her it was. She *loathed* it!

'So am I.' Gideon began to pace the room. 'Unfortunately Newman hasn't been able to find another job, either, since being so suddenly "let go" from his last one.'

Considering that Newman had been involved in an affair with his boss's wife, that 'letting go' wasn't so surprising!

'I hope you aren't expecting me to feel sorry for the man,' Joey snorted. If it hadn't been for Gideon's involvement, Stephanie might have been damaged professionally as well as per-sonally by being wrongly accused as 'the other woman' in the divorce. 'As far as I'm concerned, hanging, drawing and quartering wouldn't be enough retribution for the extent of his deceit!' Joey announced forcefully.

'Remind me never to get on the wrong side of you,' Gideon murmured.

She smiled. 'Too late!'

Gideon found himself returning the easiness of that smile. 'I'm afraid if you want to eat this evening we'll have to send out for something. I rarely eat at home,' he explained, 'so there's nothing in the kitchen apart from—oh…a loaf of bread, some butter, milk to put in tea and coffee, and maybe a few eggs. And a packet of smoked salmon,' he remembered belatedly. 'My mother brought it down for me from Scotland last week.'

Joey looked amused. 'Must be nice to have smoked salmon brought down from Scotland, or to be wealthy enough to order a takeaway or eat out every night.'

It could be a little tedious, as it happened, Gideon recognised with a frown. He hadn't realised the limitations of his chosen lifestyle before Joey had breezed into his life almost a week ago. He'd ceased to notice the cold sterility of his apartment, the impersonality of eating out at the usual restaurants four or five nights a week. Unless he was actually seeing someone, it hadn't even bothered him that he often dined alone; the management and staff of all those restaurants recognised and spoke to him, so what did it matter if he ate alone?

But bringing Joey here, seeing his apartment through her eyes, made Gideon all too aware that the lack of any personal items or photographs, and the monochrome decor, gave it all the warmth and appearance of a hotel rather than a home.

But it had been deliberate, he reminded himself impatiently. As a child, he'd had years of shunting backwards and forward between his mother's home in Edinburgh, his father's estate in Gloucestershire and the boarding school he'd attended in Shrewsbury, and then he'd had several temporary digs in London during his student years. All of which had resulted in him keeping his personal possessions to a minimum, on the basis that it was easier that way when he needed to transport them to wherever he lived next.

Gideon just hadn't realised until now that those personal possessions were almost non-existent...

'Did it ever occur to you that I can't cook, either?' he rasped.

'Surely I didn't hear you correctly?' Joey taunted. 'I'm sure I couldn't have heard the self-sufficient Gideon St Claire admit that there's something he can't do proficiently, if not better than the next man?'

Gideon frowned. 'I have no idea where you gained this impression that I'm somehow all-powerful, Joey, but I can assure you that there are a lot of things I can't do—proficiently or otherwise.'

She gave him a searching look, recognising from his closed expression that, although it had been his decision that they come back to his apartment, he was far from comfortable with allowing her this window into his private life.

'I'm feeling better now, so maybe I should just go.'

Gideon scowled darkly. 'Go where?'

Her brows rose. 'Home, of course.'

'I don't think that's a good idea.'

Joey blinked. 'Sorry?'

'I'm sure you noticed the doorman downstairs when we arrived, to screen non-residents? The security code to enter the lift? The cameras inside the lift and on individual floors?'

Joey's stomach did a lurching somersault as she began to have a dreadful inkling of exactly what Gideon was about to say. 'Yes...'

'I think, until the Newman situation has been sorted out, that it would be better if you stayed here with me.'

'No way!' Joey surged to her feet even as she frantically shook her head in protest. 'I've already had to put up with you following me about all day—'

'It works in reverse as well, you know—I've had to put up with following you about all day!' he retorted.

Her cheeks warmed at the rebuke. 'That was your choice, not mine.'

'I have a responsibility,' he came back icily.

'Because of Stephanie,' she acknowledged heavily. 'I'm sorry, Gideon, but there is no way— absolutely no way—that I'm going to... Look, I realise that I—that we—behaved less than discreetly this morning, but that doesn't mean I'm going to just move in here with you.'

Gideon recoiled as if a snake had lashed out

and sunk its fangs into him, a nerve pulsing in his tightly clenched jaw. 'Having you move in with me was the last thing I was suggesting.'

Obviously. He looked so horrified at the mere thought of it! 'Then what *did* you have in mind?' Joey challenged. 'That I just share your bed for the night?'

Blond brows lowered over glittering brown eyes. 'I don't think I care for the accusation in your tone.'

'Tough!' Joey snapped, and she was the one to now pace the room. 'I have no idea what you think I am, Gideon, but I'm definitely not easy.'

'Oh, I can vouch for that,' he muttered harshly.

Joey glared. 'You know exactly what I meant—'

'And you,' Gideon cut in coldly, 'are deliberately choosing to misunderstand what *I* meant!' He sighed. 'I'm not intending the two of us to share a bed. You can have the bedroom, and I'll sleep out here on the couch.' And very uncomfortable it was likely to be, too, considering it was only a two-seater sofa and he was six foot three inches tall!

But did he get any thanks for having his life disrupted in this way? Any appreciation for inviting Joey into his home when he never invited *anyone* here? Any consideration of his own discomfort?

No, all he received for his trouble was her suspicion and distrust. Which was damned insulting, to say the least!

'I'm not staying here with you,' Joey insisted.

Gideon drew in a frustrated breath. 'Then I guess I'll just have to come back to your apartment with you.'

'Any more than I intend inviting you to spend the night at my apartment with me!' Joey finished determinedly.

'I'll be sleeping on the sofa—'

'I don't care if you're sleeping outside in the hallway—the answer is still no!' she said, her voice rising in her agitation.

'And if Newman chooses tonight to decide he isn't satisfied with just damaging our property and decides to make it more personal?'

Joey looked frightened. 'You think he might become violent towards you or I?'

Gideon's mouth thinned. 'I think he's already violent—it just hasn't manifested itself yet into outright physical assault.'

Joey felt her face go pale and an icy shiver run down the length of her spine as she once again recalled Richard Newman standing close behind her in the queue at the coffee shop on Monday morning—the way he had deliberately stopped and spoken to her. As if he didn't care if she recognised him, or had perhaps even wanted her to.

Gideon regretted being quite so blunt when he saw the way her eyes now looked dark and haunted against the pallor of her cheeks. 'I didn't mean to frighten you.'

'Well, you succeeded!'

He ran a hand through his hair. 'Let's just calm this down a little, hmm?' he encouraged.

'And how do you propose we do that?' Joey asked.

'We would probably both feel better—less agitated—if we had something to eat.'

'You mean *I* would, don't you?' she challenged.

'I've yet to see you act as anything other than Mr Calm!'

Gideon refused to be distracted by her obvious determination to have another argument with him. 'If you don't feel like ordering food in then we could make scrambled eggs to go with the smoked salmon, with maybe some toast on the side?'

'Neither of us can cook, remember?'

'I believe, if you can handle putting some bread in the toaster, that my culinary skills might stretch to making scrambled eggs and opening a packet of smoked salmon,' Gideon said dryly; he had lived on eggs at one point during his student days, when his monthly allowance had run out before the next one was due. He preferred more sophisticated fare nowadays.

She raised auburn brows. 'Really?'

'I believe so, yes.'

'Perhaps you should go and change out of your work clothes before you start cooking?'

Gideon was still wearing his white shirt and the dark trousers of his suit. 'Into what? I don't even own a pair of jeans, Joey,' he explained as he saw her frown.

'Why on earth not?'

Gideon shrugged. 'I'm simply not a jeans sort of person.'

Amusement now glittered in those jade green eyes. 'In that case—lead on, MacDuff!'

Gideon was smiling at Joey's return to good humour—at his expense as usual, of course!—as he led the way to his kitchen. A kitchen, he realised uneasily, that with its black, lemon and chrome decor, and uncluttered and virtually unused work surfaces, was as impersonal as the rest of his apartment.

Which was exactly the way he liked it, Gideon reminded himself firmly. He moved across the room to take eggs, milk, butter and smoked salmon out of the fridge, suddenly uncomfortable with the idea of preparing a meal with Joey. Of preparing a meal with anyone. He rarely put himself to the bother of cooking at all—let alone for some cosy twosome with a woman he had previously considered to be both annoying and irritating.

Exactly when had he ceased thinking of Joey as being either of those things?

Oh, he was still frequently annoyed and

irritated in her company, but not in the same way he had been before; now that annoyance and irritation was directed more towards himself— for allowing his attraction to her to become such a big part of his life.

'You were right. I do feel much better now that I've eaten.' Joey sat back on the stool opposite Gideon's at the black marble breakfast bar where she had insisted they had to eat—rather than in the formal dining area of that cold, impersonal sitting room.

The two rooms of the apartment she had been allowed to see were both lacking in warmth. In fact they lacked any evidence at all of the personality of the man who actually lived here.

The top of his desk at St Claire's was kept similarly devoid of any evidence of the type of man who worked there each day. Admittedly he was working in Lucan's office at the moment, rather than his own, but earlier in the week Joey had needed to borrow a legal book from Gideon's office farther down the hallway. Joey had unpacked those boxes of personal items she had brought with her on Monday, and placed them about Lexie's office to make her feel more comfortable for the month she would be working there. But Gideon's office, where he had worked every day for years, was as lacking in any warmth, let alone comfort, as his apartment.

Who lived like this?

Well…obviously Gideon did. But *why* did he? Was it just another manifestation of that 'aloneness' that helped to keep him removed from emotional involvement of any kind?

The same aloneness that now, in his allowing Joey into his apartment at all, was in danger of being demolished?

Joey had been too distracted earlier to appreciate that fact, but…

'Please don't think that I'm ungrateful for your suggestion earlier that I stay here with you tonight.'

His mouth compressed. 'A suggestion you totally misunderstood.'

'Yes, and now I'm attempting to apologise for it,' she said evenly.

Gideon gave her an assessing, narrow-eyed look. 'Don't let me stop you,' he drawled finally.

Joey chuckled huskily. 'Aren't you supposed to be a little more gracious about it than this?'

Gideon's gaze became mocking. 'I'm enjoying the novelty of having the outspoken Joey McKinley apologise to me far too much at the moment to even attempt to be gracious.'

She grinned across the breakfast bar at him. 'I'm not sure, considering how rude we are to each other, how we ever came to be caught in such a compromising position earlier—' She broke off, her cheeks warming uncomfortably. 'What I meant to say was—'

'It's okay, Joey. I know exactly what you were trying to say,' Gideon acknowledged wearily— he had been trying to make sense of it all day himself. The only explanation he could come up with was that it had to be an attraction of opposites.

Joey was the warmth of sunshine to his cool of the moon. Was openly emotional to his icy reserve. Heatedly outspoken to his calm caution. Casually feminine—when she wasn't in work mode and presenting a much tougher look—to his stiff formality.

Opposites, indeed.

And yet their attraction to each other was most definitely still there...

He frowned. 'This morning was—'

'I hope you aren't about to insult me again, Gideon?' Joey eyed him warily. 'Because, the way I remember it, it was a mutual ripping off of clothes.'

Total opposites, Gideon acknowledged with a wince at her frankness. And yet that honesty was also commendable. It was even amusing on occasion. In fact he had found himself laughing out loud several times during the past week at some of her more candid comments.

'We didn't rip each other's clothes off—'

'As good as,' she insisted bluntly.

Gideon's mouth quirked. 'No clothes were actually ripped. And in my own defence I would like to state that I usually exhibit better control than I did this morning.'

'Oh, believe me, you give a whole new meaning to the word *control*,' she assured him.

'Which is why this morning's...lapse was regrettable,' he finished.

Joey gave him an exasperated look. 'Tell me,

Gideon, do your relationships usually last very long?'

He looked taken aback by the question. 'Sorry?'

'I asked do your relationships usually last very long?' Joey repeated unapologetically; Gideon might be as handsome as sin, and an erotically accomplished lover, but she couldn't see too many women putting up with the need he felt to analyse and dissect every aspect—particularly the physical part—of a relationship. She certainly found it less than encouraging.

Which was, perhaps, the whole point of the exercise?

Gideon frowned his displeasure. 'I have always found it advisable to be completely honest when it comes to what you choose to call "relationships".'

Joey quirked auburn brows. 'And what do you *choose* to call them?' she asked curiously.

He looked irritated now. 'An arrangement of mutual needs.'

She gave a splutter of incredulous laughter. *'An arrangement of mutual needs?'* she howled. 'It sounds more like you're discussing a business deal than a relationship!'

'Probably because that's how I prefer to think of them.'

'And how long does it usually take you to put your "mutual needs" card on the table?'

That irritation flickered again across his brow. 'I can always tell after a first date whether I want to see a woman again.'

'Go to bed with her, you mean?'

Gideon's mouth firmed. 'Yes.'

Joey stared at him in wonder. 'No wonder you're still single at thirty-four.'

'I'm still single at thirty-four, as you put it, through *personal choice*,' he bit out tightly.

'Keep telling yourself that, Gideon,' Joey teased as she stood up to begin loading the plates from their meal into the dishwasher. 'Personally, I'm surprised any woman ever agrees to go out with you a second time after you've given her your "mutual needs" speech!'

Gideon had no idea how this conversation had shifted to the way he conducted his personal relationships. Although why he should be surprised he had no idea; he could never predict or anticipate what the outspoken Joey McKinley was going to do or say next.

As demonstrated by her next statement!

'I suppose I should feel grateful that you haven't suggested having a "mutual needs" relationship with me.'

Gideon's expression became guarded. 'What would your answer have been if I had?'

She looked across at him. 'Guess!'

Gideon continued to look back at her for several long, searching seconds, knowing by the angry glitter of her eyes and the flush to her cheek, exactly what her answer would have been to any suggestion on his part that they satisfy their physical desire for each other within the guide-lines of his usual businesslike relationships.

He gave a tight smile as he stood up. 'I'm not sure your answer is humanly possible.'

She laughed softly. 'Probably not.' She straightened as she finished clearing away. 'Now, if you could just drive me back to the gym so that I can collect my car...'

'I can do that, yes,' Gideon said. 'But only if I then either follow you back to your apartment and stay the night with you there, or alternatively we both come back here.'

'Gideon—'

'It's non-negotiable, Joey,' he stated.

Joey could see and hear that in the implacability of Gideon's expression and tone. And, much as she didn't relish the idea of him spending the night in her apartment—her 'mutual need' for Gideon might just rage out of her control if she knew he was laying naked in the room next to hers!—she appreciated the offer. Even if that offer *was* being made to Stephanie's sister rather than to Joey personally...

'Fine,' she accepted finally. 'But don't expect me to play the gracious hostess and offer to let you sleep in the bed while I sleep on the sofa, because it just isn't going to happen,' she warned caustically.

Gideon gave a derisive smile. 'I never expected anything else.'

She gave a sweetly saccharin smile. 'I'm so pleased I didn't disappoint you!'

He was frowning distractedly as he went to his bedroom to collect the things he would need for an overnight stay at her apartment.

Joey never disappointed him. She surprised him, deliberately shocked him on occasion, and evoked an uncontrollable and inexplicable desire in him, but nothing she did or said ever disappointed him...

CHAPTER ELEVEN

'ARE you sure you're going to be comfortable sleeping on here?' Joey frowned down at the makeshift bed she had made for Gideon on the sofa in her sitting room; the only bedclothes she had been able to find were a spare set of sheets, two old blankets and one pillow.

'Probably not,' Gideon drawled as he dropped his overnight bag down beside the sofa, before taking his mobile and wallet from his trouser pockets and placing them on the coffee table. 'Which will no doubt make your own dreams all the sweeter as you sleep in the comfort of your bed.'

She somehow doubted that. Especially when he was only putting himself through this discomfort in an attempt to protect her. Something, despite her earlier apology, she knew she really had been less than gracious about.

'Perhaps I should be the one to sleep on the sofa, after all—'

'I'm just teasing you again, Joey.' Gideon dropped lightly down onto the sofa and grinned up at her. 'I'll be absolutely fine sleeping here.'

'If you're sure?'

Somehow, now that the time had come for Joey to go to her bedroom, she was reluctant to leave... She doubted she was going to get any sleep anyway, knowing he was only feet away. Possibly naked!

Good Lord, wasn't she a little young for hot flushes and heart palpitations?

'I'm sure,' Gideon answered gruffly. 'Just go, hmm?' he urged firmly when she still made no effort to leave.

Joey looked at him from beneath lowered lashes, noting the gold glow of his eyes—as a sign of his own physical awareness of her?— and the slight flush on the sharp blades of those sculptured cheeks. She moistened suddenly dry lips before speaking. 'I feel very guilty taking the bed and leaving you to sleep on the sofa.'

'Good.'

Her eyes widened. 'Gideon!'

He arched mocking brows. 'As I told you earlier, you have to learn to take it if you're going to give it.'

'Okay, point taken.' She nodded. 'There's coffee in the kitchen if you wake up before me in the morning, and—'

'And here I imagined you'd be bringing me breakfast in bed.'

Joey eyed him uncertainly. 'You're kidding again, right?'

He smiled. 'What do you think?'

She gave a grimace. 'I think you're going to be waiting a very long time if you expect me to bring you breakfast in bed.'

'Another of life's little disappointments.' He gave an exaggerated sigh.

Joey wasn't quite sure what to make of Gideon in this teasing mood. It was disconcerting, to say the least!

'Goodnight, Gideon,' she said stiltedly as she turned away.

''Night, Joey,' he called softly.

She closed her bedroom door firmly behind her before leaning back against it, aware that her heart was pounding, her cheeks flushed.

This was utterly ridiculous. She was twenty-eight years old, and a lawyer of some repute—not some inexperienced eighteen-year-old lusting after a man she couldn't have! Even if that last part *was* true. She *did* lust after Gideon and she knew she couldn't have him—on his terms, at least. She wasn't interested in a temporary fling just to scratch an itch.

Gideon's good humour had left him the moment Joey closed the bedroom door behind her, and he gave up all pretence of being relaxed as he stood up restlessly to begin pacing the room.

How the hell was he supposed to spend the night sleeping on the sofa when he knew that Joey was only feet away? Possibly naked!

Did she sleep naked…? Just the possibility that she might was enough to cause Gideon's thighs to harden to a throbbing ache as he imagined those lush, full breasts, her slender waist and invitingly curvaceous hips and thighs, sprawled across silken sheets—

Gideon turned sharply as he heard the bedroom door reopen, schooling his features to casual un-interest as he looked across at her enquiringly.

'I need to use the bathroom,' Joey said huskily,

and she came out of the bedroom wearing an over-large white T-shirt that reached down to her thighs.

So much for imagining her sleeping naked, Gideon mocked himself once Joey had disappeared into the bathroom down the hallway. Although the T-shirt did have a certain appeal, as it hinted at rather than outlined those softly luscious curves beneath...

Who was he trying to fool? She could have been wearing a sack and he would still have found her sexy!

"Night, again,' she murmured, her gaze averted as she went back into the bedroom and closed the door.

Gideon was once again consumed with frustrated desire as he stood in the middle of the room staring at that closed bedroom door for several long seconds. Knowing Joey was just behind that thin veneer of wood. That he now ached to kiss her softly pouting lips. To take her in his arms and mould her soft curves against his own. To caress every inch of her until she was as aroused as he was.

Oh, to hell with this!

He moved to grab his overnight bag before marching down the hallway to the bathroom. He needed a cold shower. A long—very long!—cold shower. For all the good he expected it to do...

If Joey had ever suffered a more restless night's sleep in her life then she couldn't think when. Surely nothing could ever have tormented and disturbed her as much as knowing that Gideon was asleep on the sofa in her sitting room?

She had actually got out of bed half a dozen times during the night, with the intention of either joining him on the sofa or inviting him to share her bed, her body aching, longing, to finish what they had started earlier that morning.

Somehow she had resisted each and every one of those longings. Forced herself to return to bed alone. Only to get up again minutes later when she was once again consumed with the same desire.

It was a relief when early-morning light started to permeate her bedroom curtains. A glance at the bedside clock revealed that it was almost seven-thirty. Surely a respectable—acceptable—time for her to get up?

Whether it was or not, Joey knew she'd had enough of lying in the tangle of her own bed-clothes. A trip to the bathroom to clean her teeth was in order, before she went into the kitchen and made herself a pot of tea. A *large* pot of tea!

She achieved the first of those tasks by simply not looking at Gideon as she moved quietly down the hallway, but she couldn't resist on her way back. She glanced across to the sofa, her breath catching in her throat as she saw him lying sprawled face-down on the sofa, with only a sheet to cover his nakedness. At least she pre-sumed he was naked beneath that sheet; his back was certainly bare, as were his long and muscled legs.

Joey couldn't resist padding softly over to look down at him, her fingers aching to reach out and touch the fall of golden blond hair across his forehead. His lashes were long against the hardness of his cheeks, his lips slightly parted as he breathed in and out.

If Joey bent down just slightly she could kiss those lips—

'I don't smell any breakfast cooking!' Gold

eyes gleamed at her wickedly as Gideon suddenly raised those long lashes to look up at her.

Joey almost tripped over her own feet as she jumped back guiltily. 'I thought you were still asleep!' she accused, her cheeks burning with embarrassment at being caught in the act of ogling him while he slept. Correction, while she had *thought* that he slept!

'Obviously you thought wrong.' Gideon took the sheet with him as he rolled over to look up at her. He was very aware that a certain part of his anatomy had woken up before the rest of him, and that looking at a sleep-tousled Joey was only increasing that throbbing ache between his thighs.

A fact she was also aware of if, the way her eyes had widened as she glanced at that restless bulge beneath the sheet was any indication!

'What can I say? Part of me is very pleased to see you,' Gideon drawled ruefully.

Joey's cheeks were still flushed, but she quirked mocking brows. 'And how does the rest of you feel about it?'

Gideon put an arm behind his head as he relaxed back on the pillow. 'As I said, I don't smell any breakfast cooking.'

Just as he had thought, sleeping on the sofa hadn't been his main problem last night. It had been forcing himself to resist knocking on her bedroom door and then joining her in bed that had proved the most difficult.

The cold shower he'd taken had been a complete waste of his time once he'd lain down on the sofa. His mind had worked overtime as he'd imagined kissing Joey, making love to her, having her make love to him...

One look at her this morning, red hair soft and tousled, those jade-green eyes heavy with sleep—or lack of it?—and all those erotic imaginings had returned with a vengeance.

'And, as I told you last night, you won't either,' Joey assured him. 'There's toast or croissants in the kitchen if you're hungry, so just help yourself.' She turned away.

Gideon reached out and lightly grasped her wrist. 'Where are you going?' his voice was husky.

She was very aware of his fingers curled lightly about the slenderness of her wrist. Of his nakedness beneath the thin sheet. Of the long length of his arousal poised beneath that sheet...

She swallowed hard. 'I thought I'd go into the kitchen and make some tea and coffee.'

Gideon gave a light tug on her wrist. 'Weren't you about to kiss me good morning a few minutes ago?'

Her eyes widened in alarm as she realised how easily she had given herself away. A sudden but unmistakable sexual tension filled the room...

'Don't be ridiculous—'

'Don't lie to me, Joey. Or yourself,' he added softly.

Joey tried to back away. 'I'm not lying—'

'I think you are.'

'No—'

'Yes!'

Gold eyes blazed up at her as Gideon's fingers tightened about her wrist before he gave a second, harder tug, and succeeded in unbalancing Joey.

She could feel herself starting to panic as she tumbled towards him. 'Stop this, Gideon,' she instructed firmly as she tried to regain her balance, but instead she found herself sprawled on top of him, only the thin material of the sheet and her T-shirt between them.

Which was no barrier at all. Joey felt the hardness of his shaft pressed against the softness of her thighs, her breasts crushed against his chest, and their faces were now only inches apart.

She lay unmoving, not breathing, as her body was suffused with heat. That heat was centring, pooling between her thighs as the intensity of his golden eyes held her captive. 'I don't think this is a good idea, Gideon,' she said.

He released her wrist to bring his hands up and cradle either side of her face, thumbs moving lightly against the shadows beneath her eyes. 'Did you sleep at all last night?'

'I—no, not really,' she acknowledged with a grimace.

'Neither did I,' he admitted quietly.

The tip of her tongue moved nervously across the sudden dryness of her lips. 'This isn't the answer, Gideon.'

He gave a rueful smile. 'Well, it certainly isn't the question!'

Joey breathed shallowly. 'Then what is?'

Those golden eyes held her mesmerised. 'The question is, can either of us stop what happens next?' Gideon shifted slightly, nudging her thighs apart. Her core was now pressed against his unrelenting hardness. 'Can you?' His hips flexed to rub that hardness against her already throbbing nubbin.

Joey gave a little whimpering moan, her eyes closing as pleasure coursed through her. She felt herself start to moisten between her thighs, her nipples peaking, hardening to an aching throb.

'Joey?' Gideon prompted throatily.

She raised emerald-bright eyes. 'Can *you*?'

Gideon shook his head. 'I don't even intend to try,' he admitted gruffly, knowing he had lost this particular battle the moment he'd heard her leave her bedroom earlier. He'd watched from between narrowed lids as she'd moved stealthily down the hallway to the bathroom, her breasts twin peaks beneath her T-shirt, her legs bare and silky. Knowing she was completely naked beneath that inadequate garment had only made Gideon desperate to remove it.

He did so now, and her thighs straddled his as he sat her up, slowly lifting that T-shirt, revealing auburn curls between the slim thighs that he longed to plunder, the slenderness of her waist, and finally the full thrust of her firm breasts, tipped with dusky rose nipples that were already pouting at him, begging to be kissed.

Gideon's gaze held hers captive as he parted his lips to reveal the soft moistness of his tongue and the sharpness of his teeth. 'Bend down and put your nipple in my mouth, Joey.'

Every breath she took lifted her breasts in invitation. Her nipples were so hard and aching now they were almost painful. A pain that she knew only Gideon's waiting tongue and teeth could assuage.

Her position of power was too much temptation, her need too great, too immediate, for her to do anything other than what he asked. Her hands moved to rest on the pillow either side of his head as she lowered her breasts and instantly felt the sharp sting of pleasure as he took one of those fiery tips deep into the heat of his mouth, while his hand cupped its twin to allow his fingers and thumb to pluck and roll the hard and aching nipple.

Moisture flooded again between Joey's thighs

and she moved against him restlessly. Gideon groaned low in his throat even as he continued to pay attention to first one nipple and then the other, teeth gently biting, tongue rasping, driving her higher and higher towards the release that was becoming a desperate need.

'I've waited so long for this,' Gideon gasped as he kissed his way across the slope of her breast before moving up to capture her lips with his.

They kissed long and deeply, desire blazing, heightening their senses to fever-pitch.

'I can't wait any longer. I need to be inside you now.' He moved quickly, rolling to his side with Joey beside him as he threw the sheet aside, before moving up and over her to hold himself poised above her parted thighs, his face savage. 'Take me in, Joey!' he urged fiercely, his lips against her throat as his hands cupped her bottom, preparing her to receive him.

Joey needed Gideon inside her just as much as he wanted to be there. Her fingers were a light grasp around him as she reached between them to guide him, groaning low in her throat as she felt him carefully enter her before sliding deeper, stretching her, filling her inch by pleasurable inch.

Joey stiffened briefly in pain, her fingernails digging into the flesh of Gideon's shoulders, when she felt his hardness surge past the barrier of her innocence to fill her totally as he buried himself to the hilt before becoming strangely still, unmoving.

'Gideon?' she prompted uncertainly when he continued to lie there.

'What the hell—?' Gold eyes glittered dangerously, and there was a flush to his cheeks as he raised his head to look down at her. 'Damn it—tell me I'm not your first lover!'

Joey felt her heart plummet even as she knew her face paled at the accusation she could read so clearly in Gideon's expression. 'I— Does it matter?'

Did it *matter*? Gideon's shattered thoughts echoed chaotically.

Did it matter that Joey had been a virgin? Did it matter that he had just ripped through the gossamer barrier of her innocence? Did it matter that, virgin or not, he had obviously hurt her? Hell, yes, it *mattered*!

His expression was fierce as he took her by the shoulders. 'You can't possibly be a virgin!'

'Well...not any more, no,' Joey acknowledged softly.

Gideon growled low in his throat as his thoughts became even more disjointed. 'But everyone knows—you and Pickard. The two of you were seen together for months!'

She shook her head. 'I already *told* you. We were *never* lovers.'

'But you must have been out with other men over the years?' he persisted disbelievingly.

Had Joey ever suffered through such an embarrassing conversation in her life before? Somehow she doubted it very much!

They were both completely naked, his hardness still buried deep inside her, and he wanted to talk about why she hadn't been to bed with any of the other men she had dated. It could only happen to her!

She moistened dry lips. 'Could we talk about this later, do you think, Gideon?'

His face darkened angrily. 'We'll talk about it *now*!'

Joey couldn't quite bring her gaze up to meet

the glittering gold of Gideon's accusing eyes. 'It's a little…awkward at the moment, don't you think?'

He wasn't capable of thinking at all right now. Was too stunned, too shocked by the discovery of her previous physical innocence, to think coherently. It was a bewilderment his manhood obviously echoed as he felt himself softening in readiness for withdrawal. Taking his previous desire to its conclusion was the last thing on his mind right now.

Gideon moved up and away from Joey, to stand beside the sofa and look down at her. She quickly pulled the sheet over her nakedness. But not before Gideon had seen the telling smear of blood between her thighs.

He closed his eyes briefly, before turning away to run his hand through the thickness of his hair. He really had just taken Joey's virginity. Indisputably. Irrevocably. Unknowingly.

But *she* had known…

Gideon turned to look at her through narrowed lids. 'None of this makes any sense.'

Joey looked up at him. 'None of what?'

'You. Me. The fact that you were still a—a—'

'A virgin,' Joey finished helpfully—Gideon still seemed to be having trouble with the concept.

'Yes!'

What had she expected? Joey wondered wearily. That the two of them would make love and it would all be wonderful?

Well, until Gideon had discovered her virginity it *had* been wonderful!

Then it had turned into something of a nightmare because of his shock. His anger.

And Joey's own realisation that she had fallen head over heels in love with him...

CHAPTER TWELVE

HER eyes narrowed. 'Exactly what is your problem with us having made love, Gideon?' she questioned slowly as he turned away to pull on a pair of black figure-hugging boxers.

He was still too stunned to know what he was thinking, let alone what was coming out of his mouth. A part of him felt as if he was burbling a lot of nonsense—and the rest of him knew that he was.

How could this possibly be? Joey was a sophisticated twenty-eight-year-old woman who gave every impression of being worldly-wise. Damn it, how *could* she still be a virgin?

And yet she was.

Had been...

And Gideon had no idea how he felt about it.

The wary expression on her angrily flushed face told him that perhaps he should keep his mouth shut until he *did* know.

'Joey—'

'I would rather you didn't, Gideon,' she warned evenly, and she moved to the end of the sofa when he would have reached out to her, all the time clutching that crumpled sheet in front of her, the knuckles of her hands gleaming white beneath her skin.

Gideon's hand fell back to his side, a scowl darkening his brow at her rejection of his touch. 'I'm not going to hurt you—well, no more than I already have.' He gave a pained frown. 'If I'd known—'

'I really don't want to talk about this any more, Gideon.'

'It doesn't just come down to what *you* want—'

'As far as I'm concerned, that's exactly what it *does* come down to!' Her eyes flashed a warning as she stood up to wrap the sheet tightly round her. 'I'm going to take a shower now. My advice to you is to leave before I come back.'

'You know I can't do that,' he rasped. 'Not with Newman rampaging about.'

Joey eyed him scathingly. 'He's hardly *rampaging*, Gideon. And even if he were I have no intention of going out today—so there's no problem, is there?'

No, the problem appeared to be totally between the two of them. And Gideon knew that he was the one responsible for it. If he had only reacted differently once he'd realised… But how could he be expected to have done that when he had been shocked to his very core by the discovery of her innocence?

'Why has there been no one else for you, Joey?' he asked quietly.

She regarded him pityingly. 'Well, Gideon, that really isn't the right question to be asking, is it?'

'Then what *is* the right question?'

Joey gave a humourless laugh before turning to walk away. 'I'm going to take a shower. Lock the door behind you on your way out.'

Gideon gazed after her in frustration, knowing by the stiff set of her bare shoulders and the straightness of her spine, that it would be a mistake to push her any further right now.

But, damn it, he had no idea what the right question should have been!

* * *

Joey had no idea how she made it as far as the bathroom before the tears began to fall, but she somehow managed to get inside the room and lock the door firmly behind her before they cascaded hotly down her cheeks.

What a mess!

She had fallen in love with Gideon. With a man who had made it patently clear he never intended falling in love with *any* woman!

Even so, she should never have allowed things to go as far between them as they had. Should never have given in to the desire—no, the *love* that had kept her awake and wanting him for most of the night.

But she *had* given in to it—had wanted and welcomed his lovemaking only to have the whole thing fall apart when he discovered that she was a virgin. If she had known it was going to cause this much trouble then she would have made a point of losing it years ago.

No, she wouldn't. She and Stephanie had grown up in a loving family. Their parents were even more in love with each other now than they had been on their wedding day. And somehow that love and total commitment to each other had become a part of both Joey's and Stephanie's psyche—so much so that neither of them was willing to settle for anything less. To the extent that going to bed with a man they weren't in love with had become complete anathema to both of them.

Well, Joey had realised she was deeply, irrevocably in love with Gideon—she had just overlooked the fact that he wasn't in love with her too. In fact she had made a complete mess of things. To the point where she wasn't sure how she was even going to face him again, with the knowledge of her lost virginity hovering between them like some ghostly spectre.

It was small comfort that he was so out of touch with emotion that he obviously had no idea she was in love with him—that the question he should have been asking was why had she chosen *him* to be her first and only lover?

Gideon was still here. That was Joey's first thought when she emerged from the bathroom half an hour later and caught the smell of toast and coffee coming from the kitchen.

He obviously hadn't taken her hint earlier for

what it was: a need on Joey's part not to see or speak to him again for at least the weekend. By Monday morning she might—just might—be able to face him again with some of her usual self-confidence.

As it was, it appeared that another confrontation was going to happen much sooner than she would have liked.

Her shoulders straightened determinedly as she disappeared into her bedroom to dress in faded jeans and a green jumper, running a brush lightly through the dampness of her hair, not even bothering to apply any make-up, and then marching back out to the kitchen—before she had time to change her mind.

Only to come to an abrupt halt in the doorway as she saw that he had set two places at the breakfast bar. A pot of tea and one of coffee were already there, steaming, along with mugs and milk and sugar, and warm croissants and toast were arranged temptingly in a basket.

'What are you doing, Gideon?' she demanded coldly.

His expression was as guarded as her own. 'Making breakfast for both of us, of course,' he said casually as he carried the butter over and placed it on the breakfast bar with the rest of the food. He was now dressed in a brown cashmere sweater and tailored brown trousers. 'I know that you prefer tea, so—'

'You proved earlier that you don't know *anything* about me, Gideon.' Joey's teeth were so tightly clamped together her jaw ached, and her hands were bunched into fists at her sides, her fingernails digging into her palms.

There was a responding glitter of displeasure in the dark brown of his eyes. 'Obviously not,' he bit out tautly, only to give a weary sigh as she became even more tense. 'Look, I don't want to argue with you, Joey—'

'Oh, there isn't going to be time for an argument, Gideon,' she informed him. 'Because you're leaving. Right now!' She looked utterly fierce and determined. 'I gave you every opportunity to do this graciously, and just leave while I was taking a shower, but now I'm telling you outright to go!'

Gideon bit back his impatience, knowing it would only make the situation worse than it already was. If that was even possible! 'I don't want to leave things between us like this,' he explained, keeping his voice deliberately even. 'Don't you see that I need to understand why you—'

'How can you possibly begin to understand anything, Gideon—about anyone at all!—when you have all the emotional warmth of an automaton?' she said vehemently. 'Your apartment is as impersonal as a hotel suite. Your office looks like no one works there. Your personal life is just as uncluttered by sentiment. No one lives like that.'

Gideon did. Through choice. Because he had seen exactly how it had destroyed his mother to lose both the husband and the home that she'd loved twenty-five years ago. Gideon's decision never to become attached to people or things, apart from his immediate family, was based entirely on witnessing the complete devastation of his mother's life.

Nothing had changed in the years of his adulthood to shake that conviction. Except he found he absolutely hated the very thought of Joey believing he lacked emotion...

'I don't believe you can accuse me of being unemotional half an hour ago,' he pointed out.

'That wasn't emotion, Gideon. It was just a natural physical reaction between a naked man and a woman,' she dismissed flatly. 'Anyone with blood flowing through their veins has those!'

He drew his breath in harshly. 'So you're saying what happened between us earlier meant nothing to you?'

Joey stiffened as every barrier inside her, every defence mechanism she possessed, sprang into place; it was one thing for her to know she was in love with Gideon, but something else entirely for him to realise how she felt about him. She deserved to leave herself with some pride after this morning's humiliating experience, surely?

'We weren't discussing me, Gideon. And we aren't about to, either,' she added firmly as he would have spoken. 'Not now. Not ever. Now, I really would like you to leave.' Her gaze met his unwaveringly, her chin held high in challenge.

Gideon had never felt so impotent, so incapable of knowing what to do or say next. Except he knew that he had to do or say *something*. That he couldn't leave things so strained between himself and Joey.

'Why don't we just sit down and eat breakfast? You felt better last night after you had eaten—'

'Feeding me isn't going to change a damned thing this time,' Joey declared. 'Right now all I want is for you to just *go*.'

'I can't leave you like this.' Gideon's mouth firmed in frustration. 'We went to bed together this morning—'

'Technically, it was a sofa,' she cut in icily. 'And I've already told you I don't want to discuss that any further today.'

'You are the most stubborn, difficult—' Gideon broke off abruptly as he heard the ringing tone of the mobile he had left on the coffee table in the sitting room, along with his car keys. 'That could be the police with news on Newman.' His expression was grim as he brushed past her on his way out of the kitchen.

Joey breathed a little easier once she was alone. She knew another reason to avoid physical relationships in future; when love wasn't reciprocated, the conversation afterwards was just too embarrassing. In Gideon's case he wasn't even aware of the *concept* of loving someone, let alone capable of realising that she had fallen in love with him!

Joey's legs felt shaky as she moved to sit down on one of the stools beside the breakfast bar, her movements a little awkward as she became aware of the slight soreness between her thighs. Yet another embarrassing aspect of having made love with Gideon earlier. Especially as that lovemaking had been cut so unsatisfactorily short...

Was there a book on the etiquette of the morning after? Or in this case the hour or so after? Joey wondered. If there was, then she badly needed to get herself a copy! Although she doubted she would ever be in need of it again after today, so perhaps not.

'It was my mother, not the police,' Gideon said tersely as he strode back into the kitchen.

Joey gave him a sharp glance as he commenced pacing the kitchen restlessly. 'Is everything all right?'

Gideon ran an impatient hand through his hair. 'She would like me to fly up to Edinburgh for the rest of the weekend.'

Gideon was going to Edinburgh for the rest

of the weekend. Why, when Joey had told him to leave earlier—repeatedly—did that knowledge cause a hollow feeling in the pit of her stomach?

'That's nice,' she said noncommittally.

'You think so?' Gideon scowled darkly beneath lowered brows. 'She says there's something important she needs to discuss with me, and she would rather do it in person.'

'Oh.'

Gideon gave a humourless smile. 'Sounds a little ominous, doesn't it.'

Joey shrugged. 'Maybe, with both Lucan and Jordan away, she's feeling a little lonely?'

He gave a snort. 'She's hardly had time to miss any of us—she only went back to Edinburgh on Monday! Or is that just me exhibiting another example of having the emotional warmth of an automaton?'

That comment seemed to have struck a nerve, Joey acknowledged with a frown. It was true, of course, but maybe she shouldn't have said it...

Too late now!

'A weekend in Edinburgh sounds like fun.'

Gideon looked grim. 'I'm glad one of us is looking forward to it.'

'What do you mean?' Joey gave him a bewildered look.

He raised blond brows. 'You're coming with me, of course.'

'I'm——? I most certainly am not!' she assured him indignantly.

Gideon stopped his pacing to meet her gaze with his own implacable one. 'Joey, nothing that happened between us this morning changes a single thing about the Newman situation. He's still out there somewhere, probably thinking up his next malicious act, which means I have no intention of going to Edinburgh for the weekend without you.'

Joey ignored the wincing pain between her thighs as she stood up. 'And I'm certainly not going to Edinburgh with you!' She shot him an incredulous look. 'What would your mother think if I were to just turn up with you?'

'I've already told her you'll be accompanying me.'

'You've done *what*?'

Gideon shrugged unconcernedly. 'My mother is expecting both of us later this afternoon.'

'I— But— Did you tell her about Richard Newman?'

'Of course not.' Gideon looked appalled. 'There's absolutely no reason to worry my mother with any of that.'

'Then what reason did you give her for me going with you?'

Joey was the one to pace the kitchen restlessly now. Gideon was insane. He had to be. Because there was no way—absolutely no way—that she could go with him for the weekend to visit Molly St Claire at her home in Edinburgh.

'I didn't.'

'You *didn't*?' Joey squeaked. 'You just told your mother that I would be accompanying you without giving her an explanation as to why?'

Gideon looked down the length of his arrogant nose at her. 'Why should I have done?'

Well, Joey knew for a fact that if she took a man with her to stay at her parents' house for the weekend they would draw their own conclusions. 'Because your mother now has altogether the wrong impression of us!'

He didn't look at all bothered by that. 'I'll explain to her once the Newman situation has been resolved.'

'And in the meantime she's going to draw all the wrong conclusions,' Joey muttered disgustedly. 'No, Gideon, I *refuse* to go with you.'

His eyes narrowed. 'You've already told me you have no other plans for today.'

'That doesn't mean I want to waste half my day in an airport, waiting to get on a flight to Edinburgh. A flight I have no wish to take in the first place,' she snapped exasperatedly.

'There won't be any sitting around waiting for a flight, because I'm going to fly us up in the St Claire helicopter.' Gideon easily shot down that objection.

Joey abruptly stopped her pacing. '*What?*'

He gave a crooked smile at her scepticism. 'Don't worry, Joey. I assure you I have a valid pilot's licence.'

'Well, that's a relief—I thought perhaps you were going to fly a helicopter on the basis of owning a dog licence!'

'I actually don't have one of those,' Gideon drawled. 'Probably because I don't own a dog.'

Of course he didn't own a dog. A dog was a living, breathing being, in need of the love and nurturing that Gideon avoided at all costs!

Joey had a vague recollection of Stephanie mentioning something about Gideon flying her and Jordan back to London last year, from the St Claire estate in Gloucestershire, after there had been a health scare concerning Molly St Claire. A scare that had been alleviated once Molly had visited a specialist in Harley Street. Which was probably why she had completely forgotten that Gideon could fly...

She remembered with a vengeance now, though—and Joey had no intention of flying anywhere in a helicopter!

'Sorry, Gideon, but you can count me out.'

'If you won't agree to go, then I'm not going either,' he said, just as determinedly.

Her cheeks were flushed with temper. 'You're being totally childish about this.'

'Either we both go or neither of us does,' Gideon repeated grimly. 'I'm not leaving you here unprotected, Joey, and that's the end to the subject.'

'In your opinion!' She faced him challengingly. 'Which means diddly-squat to me!'

'I take it that's a euphemism for you not caring for my opinion?' He arched mocking brows.

'You can take it to mean what you damn well please,' Joey told him heatedly. 'I've said I'm not going to Edinburgh with you, and that's the *end of the subject* as far as I'm concerned!'

CHAPTER THIRTEEN

'YOU can either wipe that smugly superior smile off your face, or I'm going to take it off for you!'

A statement that achieved completely the opposite effect on Gideon as he now felt an uncontrollable urge to laugh.

Joey had been utterly resentful as she threw some clothes into a bag, and bad-tempered when Gideon drove them to the private airfield where he kept the helicopter. She had maintained a stubborn silence during the flight up to his mother's home just outside Edinburgh, and been stoically tight-lipped as he'd set the helicopter down on the custom-built pad in the extensive grounds. That resentment had now finally turned to belligerence as they walked the short distance to the house.

She had eventually given in with bad grace and agreed to accompany him to Scotland, after all—but only, she had assured him firmly, because his mother so obviously wanted to see him. Gideon had so far managed to resist commenting on any of Joey's moods. Obviously she had taken exception even to his silence!

'It's not smugness, Joey,' he told her. 'I'm just relieved to find there wasn't any snow and we could land safely.'

'Was it ever in doubt?'

Gideon shrugged. 'It's February in Scotland.'

Joey gave him a sceptical glance, not fooled for a moment by his excuse; there had been a definite air of smugness about him from the moment she had agreed to come to Edinburgh with him after all. A decision she certainly hadn't made for Gideon's benefit; if Joey had her way she wouldn't see him again until she was old and past caring for or responding to him!

But Joey had liked Molly St Claire from the moment she'd met her at Stephanie and Jordan's engagement party. Molly's love and pride in her three sons had been obvious, and it was a love and admiration that was reciprocated; the three St Claire brothers obviously adored their beloved mother.

The fact that Molly had so unexpectedly asked Gideon to visit her in Edinburgh this weekend was unusual; Joey knew from Stephanie that the older woman simply wasn't one of those clingy, suffocating type of mothers. Gideon's stubbornness in refusing to visit his mother unless Joey accompanied him had placed her in a difficult position. One that, despite her protestations, she had known could ultimately have only one solution.

Which was why she was now in Scotland, approaching the huge oak front door of Molly's manor house home, with Gideon strolling along casually—and triumphantly, damn him!—at her side.

Explaining exactly why she was here with him was Gideon's problem, she had decided when she'd agreed to accompany him. And if he thought his mother wasn't going to demand an explanation at some point then he was in for a surprise!

'Now *you* appear to be smiling smugly.'

'Do I?' Joey glanced sideways at Gideon. Both of them were wrapped up warm against the cold, Joey in a thick duffel coat over her jumper and denims, Gideon in a fine woollen caramel-coloured coat over his jumper and trousers. 'I can't imagine why.'

Neither could Gideon. But he had no doubt it would involve laughing at him in some way.

Joey was back to being her normal perky, outspoken self, he realised ruefully. Almost as if their making love this morning had never happened. As far as Joey was concerned perhaps it hadn't…

Gideon wasn't having the same success in blocking the vividness of those memories from his mind as she appeared to be. In fact he had thought of little else since it happened.

He most especially wondered what the 'right question' should have been…

If Gideon were the sort of son who confided in his mother then he might have discussed it with Molly. No, he probably wouldn't; he didn't exactly feature in a good light in what had occurred!

It was frustrating as hell, for a man who was always in control of every aspect of his life, not to know what was going on. Although he should be used to it by now; Joey had had him wrong-footed in one way or another since the moment he'd first met her!

And yet Gideon knew that he was enjoying having her with him. That, bad-tempered or otherwise, he was never bored in her company. In fact—

'Gideon!' His mother had opened the door before they could even attempt to ring the bell— evidence that she had been looking out for them. She gave Gideon a brief hug. 'And Joey,' she added warmly as she clasped both Joey's hands in hers. 'Do come in and warm yourselves by the fire. Did you have a good flight?' she asked once they were in the hallway taking off their coats.

Joey shot Gideon another sideways glance before answering dryly, 'Not having flown in a helicopter before, I have nothing to compare it with.'

'Oh, Gideon is a very good pilot,' his mother said with an affectionate smile in his direction. 'I have everything ready for tea, if you would like to come through to the sitting room?'

Gideon's mother couldn't have been more welcoming, and yet Joey still felt uncomfortable about being here. 'It's very kind of you to invite me to stay, too, Mrs—er...' Joey gave an awkward wince at her inability to address Molly St Claire, who had divorced her husband twenty-five years ago.

'Please call me Molly,' she invited with a smile—a beautiful woman in her late fifties, with dark shoulder-length hair that was inclined to curl, and warm brown eyes. Gideon's eyes...

'Shall I take our bags upstairs before we have tea?' Gideon asked. He was somewhat surprised, considering the urgency he had sensed in his mother's request that he come to Scotland as soon as possible because she had something important she needed to discuss with him, that she seemed so relaxed.

'Oh, yes—do,' Molly answered. 'I wasn't quite sure what to do regarding sleeping arrangements for the two of you, so I've put you both in the blue bedroom for now, with the option that one of you can move into the adjoining room if that's what you would prefer.'

If Gideon had expected Joey to be embarrassed by his mother's assumption that the two of them would be sleeping together, then he was sadly disappointed. Instead, Joey looked fiendishly delighted as she turned to look at him with a pointedly mocking expression in those cat-like green eyes.

Gideon's mouth thinned as he turned to answer his mother. 'I'll put my things in the adjoining bedroom.' He marched out of the room without so much as a second glance in Joey's direction.

'Did I say something wrong?'

Joey felt a certain amount of sympathy for Molly's obvious bewilderment at her son's behaviour. 'Much as I enjoy seeing Gideon less than his usual confident self, I think you should know that he and I aren't a couple,' she said.

'You aren't?' The older woman looked disappointed. 'Why aren't you?' She rallied briskly. 'It seems to me that you're exactly the type of young woman to shake my son out of his complacency.'

Joey chuckled softly. 'Oh, I definitely rattle the bars of the comfortable cage he's created for himself.'

'Then might I suggest you keep on rattling them until the cage falls apart completely?' Molly advised.

Joey grimaced. 'I could be old and grey by the time that happens.'

Molly moved forward to briefly squeeze her arm. 'I love all my sons equally, Joey, and have every confidence that Lucan and Jordan have made wonderful marriages—marriages that will last and blossom. But I do worry so about Gideon—he was a very loving little boy, you know.'

Joey couldn't imagine it. Actually, yes, she could... She could almost see Gideon as a golden-haired little boy, his eyes glowing gold with happiness rather than anger, knowing he was loved as much as he loved, his world totally secure...

'He was the closest to Alexander. My ex-husband,' Molly provided unnecessarily; Joey was well aware of who Alexander was. 'When the marriage disintegrated...' She shook her head sadly. 'All the boys were devastated, but Gideon was hit the hardest. It's made him very suspicious of love, I'm afraid.'

Joey was aware that it wasn't only love Gideon was suspicious of—it was any and all emotion.

'You really are mistaken about the two of us, Molly. We're not together in that way.'

'Don't give up on him, Joey,' the other woman urged huskily as Gideon could be heard coming back down the stairs. 'The fact that he brought you here with him is significant, you know.'

Joey shook her head. 'There is a reason for that, and it isn't the one that you think—' She broke off as Gideon came back into the room.

His eyes narrowed guardedly as he moved past them to stand in front of the fire to warm himself.

'Would you mind if I gave tea a miss and went upstairs to rest instead?' Joey ignored Gideon and spoke to Molly. 'I didn't sleep too well last night and I'm feeling a little tired.' She also thought it would be better if she made herself scarce so that mother and son could have their talk...

'Of course.' Molly smiled warmly. 'Gideon, would you—?'

'I'm sure I can find my own way if you just give me directions,' Joey said, deliberately avoiding Gideon's gaze as she sensed rather than saw his amusement at her remark about not having slept well. Let him be amused; he was only feeding his mother's curiosity, if he did but know it!

But Gideon wouldn't know it. Because Gideon never thought in terms of real relationships with women. Only those relationships of 'mutual needs' that Joey wanted no part of.

'It really isn't that bad, Gideon.' Joey looked up at him with concern as he stood so tall and remote in the hallway outside her apartment, after their return to London late on Sunday afternoon.

Gideon looked down at her blankly. 'Sorry?'

'I thought Angus Murray seemed like a nice man when we met him at dinner last night,' Joey said. 'And he obviously adores your mother.' She smiled at him encouragingly.

To Gideon's surprise the news his mother had wanted to share with him was of her intention to marry a laird of the clan Murray—a man she had met at a dinner party a year ago. Angus Murray had an estate near Inverness, and the wedding was to be in the summer, after which Molly intended moving to Angus's home in the Highlands.

Joey and Gideon had met the older man the

evening before, when he'd joined them for dinner—a bluff, gruff Scottish widower in his early sixties, with admiration and love for Molly shining brightly in mischievous blue eyes.

Gideon realised that Joey had the impression he had a problem with his mother's intention to remarry, but she couldn't have been more wrong; he was more than pleased that after twenty-five years of being alone his mother had finally found someone she loved, who obviously loved her in return, and with whom she wanted to spend the rest of her life.

It was the fact that his mother, after all these years, felt *able* to love again, to make a future with another man now that the past had finally been laid to rest with Lexie's marriage to Lucan, that had thrown Gideon's own years of cynicism towards love and emotion into question.

He nodded. 'They make a great couple.'

'They do. And the fact that the police telephoned this morning and told you they have Richard Newman, and that he's admitted the vandalism, means you no longer have to feel obliged to spend any more time with *me*,' Joey pointed out happily.

Ah.

Now, *that* was a problem for Gideon.

In fact he had thought of almost nothing else since receiving that call from the police...

'What do you think will happen to him?' Joey prompted wistfully; Newman was currently 'helping the police with their enquiries'.

Gideon shrugged. 'He'll probably end up seeing the same psychiatrist as his ex-wife.'

Joey grimaced. 'There you go—yet another example of what marriage can do to you!'

'What a *bad* marriage can do to you,' Gideon corrected.

'I didn't think you were aware there was even a distinction?'

He gave a rueful grimace. 'Maybe the obvious happiness of the rest of my family has changed my mind.'

'I somehow doubt that,' Joey dismissed lightly. 'Still, the main thing is that the Newman situation is over.'

Gideon had believed he would feel relieved when his enforced time with Joey came to an end. Had thought he wanted nothing more than to get back to his own ordered life. That, once the situation with Newman was settled, he would be more than happy to walk away from her.

In fact, he didn't feel any of those things...

Gideon had no idea exactly what it was he was feeling, but it certainly wasn't the relief he had expected.

'I'll see you at work tomorrow, then.'

Gideon refocused on Joey, not in the least reassured by her wary expression as she looked up at him. He had been proved wrong, time and time again about his first—and stubbornly held—impression of her as being a hard-mouthed sophisticate who'd had any number of sexual partners. An impression he now knew to be totally wrong because she had been a virgin until yesterday morning.

'Gideon?'

He blinked as he shook himself out of his own thoughts. 'Yes, no doubt we'll see each other at work tomorrow.'

Joey had no idea what he had been thinking about just now, when he'd frowned so darkly, although she could guess: he was obviously still troubled by his mother having announced that she was to remarry in the summer. Joey knew from that brief conversation with Molly yesterday, while Gideon took the bags upstairs, that with Jordan and Lucan now married and starting out on new lives together with the women they loved, Gideon was Molly's main concern.

Although the other woman's hopes of a relationship developing between Joey and Gideon were pure fantasy!

She turned and entered her apartment. 'Goodnight, then.'

'Joey...'

'Yes?' She looked up at him quizzically, the door already half closed.

Gideon drew in a harsh breath, not sure what he was doing, only knowing that he didn't want to say goodbye to her just yet. That he didn't want to say goodbye to her at all! 'I hope you'll have a better night's sleep tonight.'

Joey gave a rueful smile. 'All that clean Scottish air knocked me out for eight hours last night.'

'Still...'

Why didn't Gideon just go? Joey wondered, knowing that if he didn't do so soon she was going to be tempted into giving in to the impulse she felt to invite him into her apartment. Into her bed! An invitation that would only end up in her feeling totally humiliated when Gideon refused…

'Drive safe,' she told him lightly.

'Do you want me to pick you up in the morning?'

'Gideon, will you just go?' Joey finally snapped. 'The strain of us having to be polite to each other for the past twenty-four hours for your mother's benefit is definitely starting to get to me—even if it hasn't got to you!'

Of course it had, Gideon realised. What could he be thinking of, trying to delay their parting in this way?

For once in his life he wasn't thinking, only feeling, he acknowledged wryly. Quite what the reluctance he felt to go back to the cold impersonality of his own apartment told him, he still wasn't sure…

His mouth twisted. 'In that case I should thank you for so successfully keeping your aversion to spending time in my company from my mother.'

'You should, yes.' Joey looked up at him quizzically. 'Well?' she prompted as he remained silent.

Gideon smiled tightly. 'That is all the thanks you're going to get, I'm afraid.'

Joey gave an answering small smile. 'Goodnight, Gideon.' She closed the door decisively in his face.

Only to sit down abruptly on the sofa once she reached her sitting room.

The strain of having been constantly in his company for the past forty-eight hours had not arisen from being with him at all—she loved being with him—but from having to hide the love she felt for him…

CHAPTER FOURTEEN

'*GIDEON, it's two o'clock in the morning!*' Joey stared up at him disbelievingly, having opened her apartment door in answer to the doorbell ringing and once again found him standing outside in the hallway.

'Yes.' He didn't even bother to glance at the watch on his wrist to confirm the time.

He was still dressed in the black jumper and trousers he had been wearing earlier, with blond hair seriously tousled—as if he had been running agitated fingers through it constantly for the whole of the last eight hours.

In contrast, Joey was wearing another overlarge T-shirt to sleep in, of pale green this time. Not that she had actually been asleep when Gideon pressed so persistently on her doorbell, but that wasn't the point. At two o'clock in the morning, he had to have *known* she would have already gone to bed.

'Gideon—'

'Why me?'

Joey blinked. 'Pardon?'

'The question I should have asked you yester-day morning was why me?' he repeated, dark eyes compelling. 'Why choose *me* as your first lover?'

Joey felt the colour drain from her cheeks, and she leant against the edge of the door as her knees felt weak. 'Couldn't this have waited until morning?'

'No,' Gideon said determinedly, and he stepped forward into the apartment before firmly moving Joey away from the door and closing it behind him. 'Why me, Joey?' he prompted again huskily.

She swallowed hard. A lump seemed to have lodged in her throat, and her lips felt stiff and un-yielding. The chances of him ever realising what question he should have asked yesterday morn-ing had been pretty slim in her estimation. She wouldn't have mentioned it at all if she hadn't believed that.

She moistened the dryness of her lips. 'Well, I had to start somewhere—'

'Don't!' Gideon rasped harshly, and reached out to firmly grasp the tops of her arms, that compelling dark gaze holding hers captive. 'You're twenty-eight years old, very beautiful, with a keen sense of humour, fun to be with—'

'Much as I'm enjoying this paean of praise, Gideon—'

'So why, when dozens of men must have wanted to make love with you,' he continued, talking over Joey's attempt at mockery, 'did you wait until I came along to make love for the first time? With a man who more often than not annoys you intensely?'

This was a continuation of her nightmare, Joey decided. She had fallen asleep after all, and this was a really bad dream. A very realistic bad dream, admittedly—Gideon's fingers felt firm on her arms, and she could feel the warmth of his breath ruffling her own tousled hair—but he couldn't possibly really be here in her apartment at two o'clock in the morning—nor could they be having this conversation!

'I think it's probably overstating it slightly to say that dozens of men have wanted to make love to me—'

'Joey, I realise this is how you normally get through your day, but for once will you just stop making a joke out of everything?' Gideon's expression was fierce as he shook her slightly.

Should she be able to feel those fingers holding her arms if this was just a nightmare? And should she be feeling slightly dazed from Gideon shaking her if she was actually asleep?

If the answer to both those questions was no, then Joey was in serious trouble!

She eyed him guardedly. 'You're really here, aren't you?'

Gideon's answer was to pull her hard against him as he lowered his lips to capture hers in a kiss that was as intense as it was punishing. His eyes glittered deeply gold when he finally lifted his head to look down at her. 'Does that seem real enough to you?' he demanded gruffly.

Yep—she was in serious, serious trouble!

Gideon gave a rueful laugh as he saw the sudden panic in Joey's expression. 'Shall we go into the sitting room and talk about this?'

'As I've already said, it's two o'clock in the morning—'

'I've already conceded that it is,' Gideon

drawled, and turned her in the direction of the sitting room. 'If you want to wait until morning to continue this discussion, then fine. I'll just sleep on the sofa again.'

'I can't possibly go back to my bedroom and fall asleep knowing you're out here on my sofa!' Joey returned sharply, obviously horrified at the very thought of it.

Gideon tilted his head in consideration. 'Why can't you?'

'Because— Well, because— You can't stay here again tonight,' she insisted firmly.

'Tell me why not?'

Her mouth firmed. 'I don't have to tell you anything except goodbye!'

'Would my telling you that I've fallen in love with you make the prospect of my staying here tonight more or less horrifying?'

Gideon held his breath, all the uncertainty, the disbelief, the fear that he had known as he'd paced his own apartment earlier, trying to make sense of his own feelings and finally succeeding, coming back with a vengeance.

What if he had totally misjudged this situation? What if the conclusions he had come to about their lovemaking yesterday were completely wrong? What if he had just made a complete idiot of himself by telling a woman who cared nothing at all for him that he had fallen in love with her?

So what if he had?

He had spent the last twenty-five years being emotionally restrained. Never really making a home out of any of the apartments he had lived in. Dressing conservatively. Driving equally unimaginative cars. Choosing friends who demanded nothing of him and women who demanded even less.

Making an emotional fool of himself was long overdue!

Although Gideon really hoped—prayed—that it wasn't going to happen with Joey...

She eyed him warily as she slowly moistened her lips again with the pink tip of her tongue. 'And are you actually telling me that? That you've fallen in love with me?' she said huskily.

Gideon returned her guarded gaze. 'Oh, yes.' The admission was accompanied by a smile, which turned rueful as he obviously saw her complete shock.

'I— But— You *can't* have fallen in love with me!' she protested incredulously. 'You think I'm outspoken. And rude. And pushy. And—'

'Yes, I did think you were all of those things.'

'But you don't any more?'

'No, I don't. What I think—know—is that I've fallen in love with you. That I want to ask you to marry me.' Gideon held his breath once more as he waited for a response.

It was that very self-consciousness that gave Joey the hope that she wasn't dreaming this after all. Surely even in a dream Gideon wouldn't look this uncertain of himself?

If not, had he really just said he was in love with her? That he wanted to marry her?

Gideon reached out and clasped both her hands in his. 'I realise this is too sudden for you—that I've done very little to endear myself to you. Hell, I've done very little to endear myself to *anyone* for the past twenty-five years,' he acknowledged in disgust. 'But if you'll let me—if you'll give me a chance, Joey—I swear that I'll do everything possible, whatever it takes, to help you fall in love with me too.'

She could only stare at him, sure that the strain of the past few days must have sent her completely out of her mind. Gideon loved her and wanted to marry her? Maybe if she kept saying it over and over again to herself she might actually come to believe it!

She swallowed hard before taking in a deep, determined breath. 'You asked why you, Gideon,' she reminded him.

'You don't have to answer if you would rather not,' he assured her hastily.

He was still massively uncertain, Joey realised wonderingly, totally incredulous that Gideon, a man always so sure of himself, was obviously completely unsure of her and how she felt about him.

Novel as that was, Joey found she didn't like it. She didn't like it at all!

'The "why you" is easy, Gideon,' she said softly. 'It's true that when I first met you I believed you to be arrogant, aloof, superior, sarcastic—'

'Stop, Joey!' he groaned.

'But I also thought,' she continued firmly, 'that you were the most gorgeous, sexy man I had ever set eyes on. I wanted us both to rip our clothes off right then and there and lie naked together on white silk sheets.'

'Red. The sheets were always red satin in *my* fantasies about the two of us,' he explained self-consciously at Joey's questioning look.

'You've had fantasies about us making love too?' Joey stared up at him in wonder.

Gideon nodded. 'I've spent the last week doing little else,' he admitted. 'In every venue and position possible—and some that probably aren't!'

'I'm shocked, Gideon!' Joey gave a choked laugh as she finally started to believe that he really *did* love her.

Gideon loved her!

He really loved her!

'No, you aren't,' he shot back.

'Well...no, not really. Perhaps *hopeful* best describes it?' Her eyes shone a mischievous green.

'Hopeful?' He looked even more uncertain.

'Gideon, haven't you realised yet that I've fallen in love with you too?' She finally allowed her eyes to glow with the emotion.

He looked down at her searchingly, wanting to believe, but afraid to hope that he really had just heard Joey say that she was in love with him. At the same time he knew that she couldn't possibly love the emotionally repressed man he had been for so long.

'Don't even try to make any sense out of it, Gideon,' Joey advised him huskily. 'I've discovered that falling in love isn't rational. Or logical. Or even sensible. It just *is*.' She gave a joyous laugh. 'And I happen to love you very, very much. So much so that if you don't soon finish what we started yesterday morning, then I really will have to start ripping your clothes off!'

Something seemed to swell in his chest—to break loose, to shatter—and as he felt his love for Joey expand and grow, filling the whole of his being, he realised that it was the shield he had always kept around his heart.

'I love you so much,' he choked out emotionally as he pulled her into his arms, burying his face in the silky softness of her hair as he held on tightly. 'Will you please marry me?'

She clung to him just as tightly. 'Maybe I should just check out that experience over stamina theory before I give you my answer?'

He gave a triumphant laugh, knowing that he

would always treasure the love and laughter Joey had so joyously brought into his life.

'Mmm, I think you might be right—experience is so much more...*delicious* than stamina,' Joey murmured a long time later, nestled in Gideon's arms, her head resting on his shoulder, in the aftermath of lovemaking beyond her wildest dreams.

He quirked blond brows. 'I'm willing to give you another demonstration if you still have any doubts?'

Joey laughed huskily, completely satiated. 'I don't,' she said softly, fingers playing lightly with the dusting of hair on his chest.

Gideon settled her more comfortably against his shoulder. 'Are you going to tell me now why you deliberately chose not to sing professionally?'

Joey's breath caught in her throat. 'You realised that, hmm?'

Gideon turned to face her and ran a finger lightly over her flushed cheek. 'You have the voice of an angel.'

'I wouldn't go that far.'

'I would.'

Joey grimaced. 'I made a promise to myself—a vow—that I wouldn't.' She shook her head. 'I loved singing. When I was younger it was my vanity, if you will. But then Stephanie was injured in a car accident when we were ten years old. She couldn't walk. And I—I made a vow that if she could just walk again—'

'You would *give up* singing?' Gideon realised incredulously. 'That is so—so…'

'Stupid?' Joey supplied ruefully.

'So typical of the warm and generous person I know you to be,' Gideon corrected. 'You were willing to give up something you loved very much if your twin could walk again.'

'Well…yes. Because I loved Stephanie more,' she explained.

Gideon had already known that from their conversation this past week. He hadn't believed he could love Joey any more deeply, but in that moment he knew he did.

'I believe it was your singing voice that I fell in love with first,' he murmured. 'When I heard that voice rising to the roof of the church at Jordan and Stephanie's wedding I really thought I was listening to an angel.'

'Stephanie asked me to sing at the wedding, and I—well, I thought that as it was for her it wouldn't be breaking my promise.' Joey smiled tremulously.

His arms tightened about her. 'Will it be breaking your promise if you sing just for me sometimes, Joey? And for our children?'

Her eyes widened. 'Our children?'

'Half a dozen of them, I think.' Gideon nodded. 'All with your beautiful red hair and green eyes.'

'If some of them are boys they might just have something to say about that!'

'They'll love you so much they won't care,' Gideon assured her indulgently.

'You really want half a dozen children?' Joey repeated wonderingly.

'Well…maybe just four—if you think six is too many?'

Joey thought six children sounded perfect— all with their father's blond hair and warm chocolate-brown eyes.

'Of course you'll have to marry me first,' Gideon insisted.

'Of course.'

'Is that a yes?'

Joey reached up to coil her arms about the bareness of his shoulders. 'That's most definitely a yes!'

There was another lengthy silence while Joey showed Gideon just how much she loved and wanted to marry him.

And Gideon immediately reciprocated by showing Joey—time and time again—just how much he loved *her*, would always love her, for the rest of their lives together.

Six weeks later

'Did I ever remember to thank you?' Gideon murmured softly.

Both Lucan and Jordan were standing beside him in the church to act as his best men, all three waiting for the moment when the organist would begin to play and Joey would enter the church, followed by Stephanie and Lexie as her bridesmaids.

Lucan raised dark brows. 'Thank us for what?'

Gideon gave a rueful smile. 'For knowing

before I did that Joey was the one woman in the world who could make me feel complete.'

His older brother returned that smile. 'She's wonderful, isn't she?'

'Well, of course Joey's wonderful,' Jordan put in. 'How could she be anything else when she's Stephanie's twin?'

'I think he's slightly biased,' Lucan murmured dryly. 'But I'm glad it's worked out for you and Joey, Gid,' he added warmly, and the organist began to play in announcement of Joey's arrival.

It had more than worked out for Gideon and Joey. The past six weeks had been the best of Gideon's life. And today was their wedding day. The very first day of the rest of their lives.

As he turned to watch the woman he loved with all his heart and soul walking down the aisle towards him, looking stunningly beautiful in her long flowing white wedding gown, and with that same certainty of love shining in her eyes only for him, Gideon had absolutely no doubt that they would spend the rest of their lives together, blissfully happy...

MILLS & BOON PUBLISH EIGHT LARGE PRINT TITLES A MONTH. THESE ARE THE TITLES FOR JULY 2011.

A STORMY SPANISH SUMMER
Penny Jordan

TAMING THE LAST ST CLAIRE
Carole Mortimer

NOT A MARRYING MAN
Miranda Lee

THE FAR SIDE OF PARADISE
Robyn Donald

THE BABY SWAP MIRACLE
Caroline Anderson

EXPECTING ROYAL TWINS!
Melissa McClone

TO DANCE WITH A PRINCE
Cara Colter

MOLLY COOPER'S DREAM DATE
Barbara Hannay